MOONBEAM

Scott M. Stockton

This is a work of fiction. Names, characters, businesses, places, events, and incidents are either the product of the author's imagination or used in a fictitious manner. Any resemblance to actual persons, living or dead, is purely coincidental.

Copyright 2017 by Scott M. Stockton

All Rights Reserved

In the desert,

not everything is what it seems.

PART ONE

SLEEP WALK

August, 1960

Roswell, New Mexico

Chapter 1

The droning sound of the typewriter's keys were now beginning to hum in Wendy's head as she finished up her report for the day. Thankfully her boss installed the new air-conditioning in his office area, and it was a little more bearable to work in the summer now. It'd been a long five hours and she was ready to go home for the night and rest. Pulling out the last sheet of paper, she cracked the joints in her knuckles as the door beside her desk opened. An older man in a brown suit and thinning gray hair walked in, directly looking in her direction.

"It's nearing 4:30 now, Miss Fields. You may leave for the day" he said politely. The young woman nodded her head gently, and breathed a small sigh of relief. Thankfully, it was also a Friday and the weekend sounded like the perfect time for peace and quiet at home.

"Thank you, Mr. Johnson" she replied, standing up and gathering her belongings. The man closed the door after a quick wave goodbye, and Wendy grabbed a Dixie cup of water on her way out. The heat of outside wafted against her face immediately. It was certainly a scorcher for a late August day, but when you lived in a desert town, the summertime is always the longest season. It wouldn't start getting cooler until late October. The sun beamed brightly off the chrome of her black and yellow 58' Dodge Sierra station wagon as she opened the door. She shook her hand lightly from the touch of hot metal and tossed her purse across the front seat. As she rolled the driver's side window down and started the engine, Mr. Johnson came running outside before she could leave.

"Miss Fields!" he called out, finally reaching her. Wendy fought the urge to roll her eyes behind her cat's eye glasses, and greeted her boss with a pleasant smile.

"Yes sir?" she asked him. Mr. Johnson stood beside the car with a hand over the roof and caught his breath.

"Your sister just phoned me" he told her. "She gave me a message to call her as soon as you get home."

Wendy's smile straightened a bit, and she nodded to him again. Just the thought of Christine always made her feel a bit tense. Considering the fact they hadn't spoken to each other for a few years now. They were never very close, and living in another state made it even harder to stay in contact with someone you don't share many memories with. Wendy hadn't realized she was sitting there in silence with the engine running and her boss made an attempt to speak again. "Are you alright, Wendy?" she asked her cautiously. Wendy blinked and then forced a smile.

"Yes, just a bit tired you know. My sister and I don't get along well, and I haven't heard from her in a while." She explained. Mr. Johnson's eyes looked away uneasily, seeming to avoid any needless drama as she stared at the sky, and back to the ground.

"Well, I just thought I'd let you know. I'll see you on Monday, Miss Fields" he said, leaving the conversation. Wendy said a quiet goodbye and drove off. She felt slightly ignored, but she wasn't going to let it get to her. After all, who would want to stand out in ninety degree weather and listen to a story about feuding siblings anyway? *"I think I'll sleep early tonight"* she thought to herself.

Walking up to her front door, the distant sound of a ringing telephone forced Wendy to unlock it faster. Rushing into the living room and dropping her purse, she answered it just in time to hear her sister's voice on the other end.

"Hey, where have you been? I've been trying to call you for hours now" she said rudely. Wendy took her glasses off and rubbed her eyes in frustration. It was a classic thing with Christine...always making things sound more dramatic than what they really were. Wendy knew she only tried calling thirty minutes ago.

"I was at work. You know...*working.* Some of us have to do it for a living, Christine" Wendy commented stressfully.

"Yeah, I called there too," Christine replied, ignoring Wendy's response, "Your boss said you left so I called your house several times."

Wendy set the phone receiver down on the table as she removed her shoes and sat on the couch slowly. She could hear her sister talking in the background, but she knew it wasn't anything important. At this point, she was probably saying how she never gets to talk with her during the day, and disregarding the fact Wendy's job demands her attention until the evening. She picked up the phone again and Christine was asking *"Are you there?"* over and over.

"Yeah, I'm here" Wendy said, leaning back against the couch. She rubbed her forehead to ease an oncoming headache.

"You were doing it again, weren't you?" Christine asked, "You put the phone down when I was talking and ignored me."

Wendy sighed and stared up at the ceiling. "I wasn't ignoring you, Christine...I was taking off my shoes. Do I have to explain everything I do?" she questioned. Christine paused for a moment and sighed heavily over the phone. It almost sounded like a short gust of wind blowing into the speaker.

"Look, I wanted to tell you that I'm getting married. Jack and I decided to tie the knot" she said finally. Wendy sat forward and raised a brow.

"Oh really now...so he finally proposed" she said, showing her disinterest.

"Yes...and I'd like for you to come to the wedding...if that's okay" Christine announced gently. Wendy closed her eyes, knowing it was leading to this. She *knew* Christine would ask her come as soon as she heard the word *"married"*.

"Christine...you know Jack and I...don't get along. You know that, don't you?" Wendy asked her. "I mean...he's never respected me, so why should I care?"

"Well that's a little harsh, don't you think? I was actually wanting my little sister to be here for me. This is...very important to me" Christine admitted. Even though she couldn't see her face, Wendy knew Christine was being serious now. She could tell by the tone of her voice. This was something meaningful to her. The situation wouldn't be uneasy, if she wasn't marrying a self important, egotistical man, but she had to admit to herself...she'd like to know Christine a little better than this. She'd like for the arguments to stop and just be sisters again. Christine went on talking after listening to Wendy's silence.

"I know you and I haven't got along very well since Mom died, but...can you just do this one thing for me? Please?" she asked again. "You don't have to stay at the house, I'll book you a hotel room, myself. You won't even have to pay for it."

Wendy tilted her head back again in thought. *"Oh, how thoughtful of you."* Even though she knew she was going to say yes.

"What time should I be there?" she said, not making it sound like a question. Christine's voice seemed to light up at the sound of Wendy's acceptance.

"The wedding is on Monday. I already asked your boss if you could take a few days off-"

"Let me handle my boss, and I'll be there by tomorrow" Wendy interrupted her. "This is kind of short notice, you know. I was planning for the weekend alone, but I think I can make the drive there by Sunday. I may need to stay at a motel along the way."

"Okay, Wendy. I hope to see you soon" Christine said, and quickly hung up the phone as Wendy replied.

"Yeah, I'll see you soon" she said. Wendy listened to the sound of the phone line hum in her ear for a minute after her sister ended the call. She slowly hung up the phone and stared at the picture of her mother on the mantle beside the deco clock above her fireplace. The fireplace she rarely used, because it never snowed in Roswell. The desert got cold at night sometimes, though. She originally grew up in Albuquerque, but moved after her mother passed. Christine met Jack and moved to Phoenix, Arizona on a whim. She always thought their relationship would never last, but now...they were getting married. Apparently, Christine was wanting to start her life now. Wendy hadn't met the right man yet. Roswell wasn't a large town, and she sometimes felt stuck there. It wasn't that she hated her location, but rather there was no one to talk to. Her high school friends all moved away, and occasionally they would call, but she could tell they were getting bored of it. Getting bored of talking with the woman who never got married. Nearing the age of thirty now, Wendy was still twenty-nine and single, but it didn't bother her like it seemed to bother other people. Being alone was nice. It was lonely at times, but also nice. No one to bother you.

She placed her hands over her eyes, and realized they were wet from tiny tears. She must've been lightly crying at her thoughts again. Sometimes that happened. Looking up at her mother's picture again, she whispered out loud to herself. *"If only you were here, Mom. You would know what to say. You always knew what to say."*

Chapter 2

Shortly after taking some aspirin, Wendy began to pack up a small suitcase for the upcoming trip. Her headache had eased away by now, and she decided to leave the same night to get a head start. The trip was close to a day and a half worth of driving, and she felt a quick sleep at a motel would be good enough until she arrived. Loading her case into the backseat of her wagon, she watched the sun setting quickly on the horizon. It was a still evening and the desert wind drifted softly. The air was getting cooler for the night now, but she left her coat at home. She'd take Route 380 out of town and head toward Las Cruces, and eventually onto Tucson, and then arrive in Phoenix. Hopefully by Sunday night. She changed her clothes for the trip after a shower, wearing a yellow and white polka-dotted dress and matching yellow heels. She gazed into her own blue eyes in the bathroom mirror, staring at her soul. She wasn't smiling, yet she felt curious about the wedding events. It occurred to her, that she didn't even know how many people would be there. She supposed, if the celebration went sour in anyway, there'd be other people to talk with at least. It was a change of pace for the time being, and maybe she'd actually enjoy it. She curled her auburn red hair into a flip style, and held it in place with a yellow headband. She smoothed on a flirtatious red lipstick, and after putting on her cat's eye glasses again, she now felt ready to go.

    The distant sky appeared crimson with an orange lining above the high clouds. The stars were peeking through them in pale glows of whitish blue and Wendy stared ahead in twilight. The darkness was heavy in the desert. So vast and long around you, making one feel alienated in a large empty world. Roads of nowhere leading far across the land of rocks and sand. The silence was deafening. Nothing but the sound of the wagon's engine as it drove along. Wendy counted the series of yellow lines on the black asphalt that faded to gray in many parts over the years of sandstorms. Through the quietness, she was beginning to let uncomfortable thoughts seep into her mind again. Reaching for radio, she figured some sound would be best for a long drive such as this. Any music would do. She just didn't want the silence.

A few clicks of static crackled through the speakers until finally a man's voice came on. He was serious in tone and she could tell it was a sudden news interruption. Turning up the volume, she heard the man warn nightly drivers of a large fogbank settling over the desert road on Route 380. Wendy was now in the long stretch between Roswell and the fork onto Route 70. It was the apparent path of the foggy weather quickly approaching. She stared at the radio with intent as the man advised all drivers to either turn back to the nearest town, or proceed with great caution. Wendy wasn't about to turn around after agreeing to the road trip, and she pressed onward toward the fork. It was then…she saw it in the distance. What appeared to be a long smoky wall, thick across the road in front of her. She slowly began to break as the wagon drove through the large fog cloud. She coasted through carefully, watching for oncoming headlights and she could barely see anything at all. The man's voice hazed out in a terrible fit of static as the signal became lost. Wendy turned off the radio, since the sound was unbearable to listen to. She felt the air inside her car drop immediately, and she noticed tiny ice particles forming on the windows. It laced itself around the windshield wipers, and grew thicker as the fog became denser. It made her mouth agape at the sight, and she whispered to herself.

"What the hell..." she breathed. Watching the ice skate over the glass, she pressed the pedal lower and the car went faster through the cloud. The quicker she got through this, the better. It seemed she would be frozen by the time she got out.

She glanced at the rearview mirror, and the small amount of light behind her had long vanished completely. The only glow was coming from her speedometer. It dimmed slightly, and the layers of fog merged into solitary blackness. She wasn't sure if she was through the cloud now or not. Everything looked the same outside the windows. A long stretch of nothingness all around her. Slowly creeping over her body and making her feel closed. She felt it hard to breathe now, taking quicker breaths and she pushed the car faster through the dark.

"I...gotta get outta this..." she mumbled, staring wide-eyed and forward. A panic was rising up her body, and the speedometer reached sixty miles per hour. Wendy took in a long breath and finally...she saw the streams of fog again rolling over the windows. The ice was beginning to melt into streams of water, and a yielding glow of blue light shown in the distance. It poked through the cloud welcomingly, and soon the gray air lifted from the car entirely. Wendy gazed through her rear mirror again, watching the fog float further and further away. The road ahead was bright. Unusually bright for the middle of the night now, and the stars appeared larger in the sky. It was amazing to see, and it made Wendy lean forward as she looked up through the windshield. She slowed the car again, and the same blue light from before now shown in front. An incandescent glow of neon lights sat on the right side of the road, coming closer as she approached. The sign sat upon a tall pole, and read *Moonbeam Diner* in large lettering. It was positioned below a sailing rocket gliding over a crescent moon. The lighting was a brilliant royal blue, somewhat cerulean in color, and accented with white neon. Below the sign sat a shiny chromed diner as it welcomed hungry travelers. It looked like a silver train car sitting on a parking lot in the middle of the desert night, merging against the sky. The stars above reflected on the exterior. It made Wendy smile as she drove her car into the parking lot. The entire diner was done in a space-age theme, and was awe-inspiring. She'd been to diners before, but not like this one. It seemed brand new and top of the line.

After parking her Dodge, she took out her purse and stared off into the distance. All around the area there was nothing for miles. An ocean of rocky desert sand and the long stretch of road. It was faint, but she swore she could still see the fog cloud back to where she came from, but the gaze was interrupted by a loud bang in the distance. Something…echoed far across the air, and it seemed to come from inside the diner. Sounding like door slamming, or something heavy dropping. It made her jump for a moment, but decided to ignore it since she knew there must be people inside. It was a comforting feeling to know that others were nearby. Oddly enough, there were no other cars in the parking lot, except her own. Possibly whoever was inside actually lived nearby, or parked their vehicle in the rear of the building. So as not to take up the customer parking spaces.

Walking up the few steps to the diner door, Wendy reached for the chromed handle and stopped. It was very slight, but she could feel a vibration in the air waving off the building. Slowly bringing her fingers to the chrome, she expected it to feel cold…but it was warm. Strangely warm. It almost felt…*alive*…to the touch. Or maybe it was just the electrical energy in the air, from all the neon piercing to the sky. The building was indeed very bright, and staring at it for too long made Wendy's eyes squint. This place was different. *Very different.*

Thinking about it as she stood there, never once had she heard of this place, nor seen it. The Moonbeam Diner was a completely new discovery for her, and yet she'd driven on this road before. A couple of times actually, while going back and forth from Roswell and Phoenix. It wasn't often she visited her sister, but she would surely remember this place. However, being so bright and new looking, maybe it truly was brand new. A recently built diner for travelers between cities. She shook her head and pushed the door open. *"You're over thinking things"* she thought. *"It's just a diner...nothing more."*

The other side of the door revealed quite a unique scene. A mode of blue and white tiles and leather, set between a radiance of chrome. A long eating counter made up the main room, facing the back from one end of the diner to the other. A series of chrome stools with blue leather seats ran along the ends. Facing toward the kitchen area behind it, closed behind a silvering door. Metallic lamps hung from the ceiling over each dining booth against the row of windows at the front end of the building. They were on both sides of the entrance where Wendy stood. To the far left side, a polished Ami-I200 jukebox sat by the wall, light blue, pink and yellow in color. On the far right end of the room were the restrooms. Wendy walked slowly to the right and sat down in the booth furthest on the end, staring at the room in amazement. Such a regal place had to be new to look this good. It truly appeared untouched for how clean it was. There was a faint smell of metal in the air, mixed with meat and grease. Presumably coming from the kitchen area. Wendy found herself feeling a bit impatient as she waited for someone to serve her. Maybe no one knew she was here, being the middle of the night. Looking down at the table in front of her, she lightly traced her finger on the moon shaped designs printed on the top.

"Well hello there..." a soft voice flowed like music from Wendy's right side. She flinched to see a tall young man standing beside the counter, legs and arms crossed as he cocked his head. He was staring gently at her with half-squinted eyes and a slow, sly-like smile. She turned her head to face him, and noticed his youthful features immediately. His platinum blonde hair curled around the ends above his forehead, looking light and fluffy. Done up in a duck tail style, dangling just above his eyes. His eyes…a vibrant green, which almost looked unnatural how they gleamed at her. A shine bounced off his pale and flawless skin tone. He looked like a painting come to life, or resembled a living doll. Wendy couldn't help but stare. He was *gorgeous* to look at. As he walked over to her, it felt enchanting the way he moved. Very quiet and sleek. He barely made a noise as he placed a napkin down on the table beside her. "Welcome to the Moonbeam Diner, Miss. My name is Johnny" he told her kindly. He seemed quite tall, but maybe it was only because she was sitting. He had to have been over six and a half feet tall, but he nearly looked eighteen or twenty years old. His height wasn't average for a boy of that age. Wendy felt herself blush as she breathed deeply. He smelled of cookies and frosting. A true dreamboat if she ever met one. She noticed his arms were rather toned as the muscles gently peeked from under his white sleeves. He was dressed in blue, same as the diner, and a white apron graced his slender hips. She found herself wondering what he must look like while naked. The sight of his bulge in those blue pants was very obvious from where he stood, and these thoughts made her feel perverted for thinking them so quickly. She swallowed hard as he handed her a menu from another table. He was bending forward just enough to make her feel body heat rise, and she liked it. In fact, she wouldn't mind him leaning closer. "What's your name?" he asked her. Placing a hand over her chest, she cleared her throat and spoke.

"I'm Wendy" she replied weakly. He reached forward and cupped her hand softly as he placed a wrapped set of silverware in her clasp.

"Well, Wendy...are you hungry tonight? I just fired up the stove. You can have anything you want" he told her. Wendy smiled shyly, and turned her head to the menu quickly, trying to hide it. Her glasses fell onto her lap and Johnny slowly picked them for her. Wendy stopped breathing for what seemed a whole minute when the young man's arm reached so close to her. She broke the silence with a question.

"I'm I... your only customer?" she asked him. Johnny's smile returned, and for second Wendy thought she could see the pointed tips of fangs peeking out below his upper lip before he answered.

"One customer is all I need tonight" he said, somewhat mysteriously, but Wendy strangely never felt threatened. His presence was warm and comforting. He truly was a charmer, or just very oblivious to how handsome he was. "You must have traveled far…to reach this crossing. I would like it very much…if you'd be my customer, Miss Wendy" he spoke again. His fanged teeth poked out again, and even though Wendy was staring straight ahead at him, his lips moved so quickly. She *still* couldn't tell if they were truly there or not. Maybe it was just how captivating he was…and he made her think unusual thoughts. Scrambling her mind, little by little in a kind and forgiving way.

"Well I am a little hungry" she admitted without turning away. Johnny's eyes narrowed when he grinned, and he opened the menu below her.

"That's wonderful. What would ya like?" he asked, making it sound more like a statement than a question. Turning her eyes to the laminated book and read the first words she saw in front of her…even if it wouldn't have been her first choice.

"Meatball soup" she said. Her response felt programmed when she spoke. "And a vanilla shake."

Johnny touched his fingertip and thumb delicately under her chin and gave a quick wink.

"Be back in a jiffy" he told her. Turning around from the table, and taking the menu back with him, he casually walked away through the silver colored door behind the counter. Disappearing into the kitchen. Wendy shook her head, and softly rubbed her eyes. She realized her glasses were still on the table, and she put them back on. She felt even hungrier than before, as though something had been draining her energy.

Chapter 3

The room was quiet again. Brightly lit and deathly silent. There was a constant humming from the neon lights above, and vibrating outside the windows. Leaning back against the seat, she stared down the room again and noticed the jukebox again. Raising a brow, and opening her purse, she found a few quarters. Walking up to the record machine, she made a glance at the kitchen area behind the counter as she walked by it. The silver door had no window, but a beam of light shown from the opposite side. She assumed Johnny was in there now, making her meal for her.

The jukebox was truly a thing of beauty, and very fancy. The chrome designs reminded her of car ornaments the way it was adorned. Looking at the song board, she made an odd discovery. Every song tag was blank. Nothing but the empty slots, which was weird to her considering just beyond the turntable she could see the record carousel. It was loaded with 45 rpm vinyls. It's obvious the machine had music in it, regardless of missing song tags. Shrugging her shoulders, Wendy placed a quarter in the slot and made a selection.

"Please be Elvis" she said allowed, waiting for the carousel to move.

It never did.

Surely, the one quarter was enough, but she placed a second one in the slot and made a different selection this time.

Nothing.

The jukebox never moved, nor made a sound. The only sound she ever heard was the quarters dropping in the bank. She folded her arms in frustration, feeling dissatisfied and turned away from the machine. "I guess I'll sit in silence then" she told herself. By the time she got back to her seat, the sudden urge to urinate struck her bladder and made her way to the door reading *"Powder Room"* on the front with the feminine symbol. Thankfully, not taking very long to relieve herself, Wendy washed her hands at one of many chromed sinks by a large wall mirror. There were even neon lights in here as well, as little white moons decorated the blue tiled walls. This place was certainly theme productive and true to its name. Thinking about the lovely Johnny again, she wondered if he owned the place or merely worked here. He seemed quite young to own a business, but maybe he'd inherited the lot from someone. Or it was a family business. It occurred to her, that she never even asked his age. It just wasn't something you ask when you first meet someone. At least, that's how she felt about it. She couldn't speak for everyone on this thought.

Wendy's reflection shown inside the mirror as she looked upon herself. From behind, there was a murky corner of the restroom that made her eyes focus on it. She squinted vaguely and for a moment she saw a pair of green orbs glowing from that corner, seeming to gape directly at her. She turned around quickly with a gasp and the lighting of diner cut out. Everything was black for only a second until the humming of the neon kicked on again. Every light shown bright and made her eyes close tightly. Opening them sluggishly, she noticed the darkened corner was empty again. Clutching the sink behind her, Wendy slowly made her way toward the door and could hear something in the dining room. It was music.

A distant melody was playing, and her first thought was the jukebox. As she opened the door, the music flooded her ears in a soft flow. It wasn't forceful, but gentle like the wind. It glided down the room artfully as the needle skated on the record. Wendy could make out the song as *"Sleep Walk"* by Betsy Brye. A rare vocal version of the song. Wendy stopped by her table as she stared down the room. The song was beautiful...yet melancholy all at once. So clear and dreamy. It made Wendy's body want to relax, but she stopped herself. It almost felt like a trance taking over her mind. She fought to keep it bay, and began to call for Johnny.

There was no answer.

The jukebox was loud, and he possibly couldn't hear her with the kitchen door closed. Why hadn't he come out yet? It was taking much longer than a jiffy, that's for sure. You'd think he'd want to check on his only customer after a power surge quaked in the building. Wendy wondered if the temporary outage was what started the jukebox and gave it a jumpstart.

She called for Johnny again, not moving from her spot, and again there was no reply. Something was beginning to feel very wrong now. She didn't think she was over thinking the situation this time.

Maybe Johnny got hurt, and the power had electrocuted him. Such a thought made her mouth open lightly as she covered it with one hand. Taking a few breaths, she took her car key from her purse and placed it in her dress pocket, just in case she needed to leave in a hurry. One may never know what will happen in a new situation. She walked over to the main entrance of the diner and pushed on it. The door wouldn't budge, and even after pulling on it, she cracked a nail when it slipped off the chrome. The door was powerfully vibrating now, and it made a rumble when she touched it. Wendy held her breath and her blue eyes grew wider. It seemed the building...*was keeping her inside.* The lock wasn't even set, from what she could see. Yet somehow the door just wouldn't open. Outside, the sky was moving quickly. The brightly glowing stars were sliding down the horizon like raindrops on glass. She backed away from the door and held her hands over her mouth. Amazed at what she was witnessing. The light beams danced across the metal body of her station wagon in the parking lot. It looked as though the sky was shifting in the night, and music only grew louder.

"What the fuck is happening..." she sputtered in a shaky voice. She wondered to herself...what kind of place she had truly come to.

Where was she in the world right now…for the sky to behave in such a way…that no one could understand. Or was this…another world entirely?

Backing to the counter behind her, Wendy startled herself and ran up to the kitchen door. She first knocked on the door rather hard, and then thought it was a stupid thing to do. It opened slightly, and she gave it a push. Peering inside, she saw no one. A small stove area was placed against the back wall, and there was a series of chrome cabinets and drawers on both sides of the room. Johnny was nowhere to be found. Walking in, her eyes shifted from side to side and she tried to find him. He'd been the only person she'd seen for miles after leaving Roswell and driving through the fogbank.

"Johnny…where are you…" she mumbled, peering around yet another corner at the far end of the kitchen. Facing the back wall on the side, there appeared to be another door down a short hallway. Wendy felt her heart beating rapidly as her hands pressed against the walls on both sides of her. There was no light, but a steady glow coming from below the door. Finally reaching the knob, she turned it carefully. As though making a sound were a deadly decision. The door barely creaked and a murky staircase emerged below her.

This was obviously the entrance to the basement storage, and remote sounds were coming from below. Deep from within the dim flame of light trickling through the darkness.

What does one do, when a situation such as this comes along and we're forced to go one way or the other? Most of us as human beings are always curious. We fear the unknown, but we wonder what it's truly like. We fear of certain death in the dark, and finding no means of escape. No one wants to die alone, and yet…we walk alone into the blackness…forever fueling our curious minds about what is truly waiting for us there. Stepping one heel of her yellow shoes on the first step made Wendy's decision. If Johnny were anywhere inside the diner…she would find him down here.

Chapter 4

With each step lowering downward, the air became heavier and hotter. There was a thick stench that coursed up Wendy's nose and she promptly covered it in disgust. She didn't speak, but moved onward until her heels tapped the bottom floor. The smell was like pennies – a warm metallic odor that stunk up the entire room. It was a terribly dark area with no sight of windows to the outside. The only light was an orange glow coming from around the corner at the far end. She couldn't tell what was on the floor, but as she walked it began to feel squishy in some parts. She could hear something wet and mushy below her steps and she occasionally lost her balance. Luckily, she'd worn high heels almost every day of her life, and was able to steady herself. Her mind was racing at the thought of what could be on the floor. She didn't want it to be something dead she was stepping on...especially when the smell in the air was getting stronger as she came closer to the light. Maybe it was garbage pilled around her, and she was stepping on insects as their guts oozed out of their bodies. She *did* think she could hear the distant sounds of little scurries moving about the room. Possibly climbing up the walls and the mysterious objects scattered here. The very thought of such things was making her stomach churn and nauseate. The smell wasn't helping either. A few times, Wendy nearly gagged quietly.

The light was just around the corner now. She could see the shape of the wall as she touched it. A black stone wall that felt sticky on her hand when she gripped the edge for balance. Quickly pulling it off, she felt a gooey substance that slimed down her fingers. It was enough to make her gag hard, nearly vomiting this time. Whatever it was, it smelled atrociously and she shook wildly before wiping it on her yellow and white polka-dotted dress. Back in the dining room above, she heard the jukebox steadily playing the same song over again. It was clear that it was all it would play. The same version of *"Sleep Walk"* with Betsy's regal sounding voice hanging in her mind. Wendy swallowed deeply as she turned the corner, her lips frowning tightly to the point where is began to ache.

Standing there...facing with his back turned to view...was Johnny.

The orange and yellow glow came from a large flame on an old-fashioned gas stove, readily burning as a large pot sat above it. It was boiling rapidly and he was stirring the liquid casually as he hummed the same tune the jukebox was playing behind her. She stared at him in surprise, widening her eyes as she noticed something *very* unnatural. It was true that Johnny was stirring the pot...but as he did so...his other arm was busy rolling wads of meat into ball shapes. They looked very reddish in color, and she noticed them oozing an even thicker red liquid. She could see it was blood rolling out of them...and one of the meaty balls held what looked to be the iris to an eyeball...peering at Wendy dead on in a horrific manner. As he picked it up, a long string dangled below it, dripping tiny droplets on the burner as they sizzled. He plopped it in the pot in a playful manner, and it vanished in the bubbles.

Wendy's hands slowly came up to her face and she stopped to find them covered in blood from when she touched the wall before. She knew now...she knew what had been happening here. Turning her eyes down on the floor...that's when she saw them. *People.* Scattered across the floor were piles of bodies...but they weren't complete. They'd been chopped and torn apart by something razor sharp. She could see the slice marks in the skin of arms and legs...heads and torsos...all lying together in rancid piles of gore and mush. They had been there for a while, since parts of the skin were now growing mold as many cockroaches ran over the severed faces. They weren't even from the same person. There were bodies of various sizes and different sexes. Several shades of skin tones were meshed together on the floor with eyeless skulls. Most appeared to be adults, but some were slightly younger. Laying just below her was a torn blue poodle skirt, shredded from all sides. No corpse was inside it, but Wendy knew it was a style of clothing favored among younger girls. Particularly teenagers. It was unimaginable at how many people could be lying dead in this room. The thought was so horrifying that Wendy finally vomited on the skirt she stared at. She was sure that Johnny knew she was here now, and she looked up at him with her eyes swelling in tears. The soup he'd been making was most likely for her, but he never turned his head. He just kept humming the song as he went to his work. Wendy gasped loudly as a shadow cast over her face from the gleaming fire. Reaching out from behind his uniform was something she'd never forget the sight of for as long as she lived.

Stretching high above his head...an elongating tentacle arm bobbed in the air as it seeped out from behind his shirt. It appeared to reach its way out of his back...and it grew thicker in mass as it moved. Whoever Johnny was...certainly wasn't something human. He was not of this world...and Wendy's mind began to shake inside. She felt her body tremble and go cold with tunnel vision at the sight of another tentacle snake its way out of his back. They opened tiny suckers on the ends, allowing slithering tongues to squirm out and breathe. Small rows of jagged teeth perked the ends, and his head turned toward the woman standing behind him. His vibrant green eyes gleamed at her with hate as he snarled deeply in his throat. His lips rolled back and she finally saw the fangs that cheerfully peeked at her earlier when they first met. Only this time, they weren't so inviting. They were long and pointed, like a vampire's teeth and when he spoke, the heat of his breath merged with the room.

"You aren't supposed to be down here, Wendy..." he warned her with a snarl. His voice was no longer elegant, and it echoed off the walls like a microphone would. It sounded robotic, yet alive and it vibrated her eardrums. Wendy's lungs were hyperventilating as she fell backwards on the slushy floor. Her tears streamed down her make-up filled face and pulled herself up to run.

"Oh my god!...." she cried out, racing toward the stairs. Her voice was feeble and strained, finding it harder to swallow and breathe. Her high heels made her feet trip on the steps, but she kept going. Ignoring the pain of a twisted ankle and she hobbled through the kitchen. Looking behind, Johnny wasn't there...but she knew he was coming...she *knew* he was coming. Whatever he...or *it* was.

Reaching to the front entrance of the diner her body collided with the chrome as it stopped her quickly. Her head banged against the glass, and she straightened herself. They were still locked in place, and it wasn't going to let her leave easily. A smooth texture wrapped itself around her leg and Johnny's tentacle pulled her body down on the floor. She knocked the contents of a nearby table off in a noisy fashion. The salt and pepper shakers shattering to pieces and the napkin holder clanging on the tile. Wendy screamed loudly as he dragged her closer. His tentacle arm squeezed tightly and stung her on her skin, tearing through her dress and pulling off her shoe. She tried grabbing something...anything...and her nails broke off when they scraped the floor. His second tentacle latched her other leg, pulling faster as she screamed the word *"no"* over and over. He was relentless, and clearly not letting up until he had the taste of her flesh in his jaws. Grabbing the napkin holder, Wendy reached around and slammed it against Johnny's head as hard as she could. It seemed to work as he let out a snarling wince and his arms let her legs go. Running for the door again, she grabbed a chair and threw it against the window until the glass shattered. Johnny reached for her again with a bleeding eye, and she threw the chair at his chest. This time he fell back, and she crawled her way out of the window to safety.

Running toward her car, she took the key out of her dress pocket from before, and started the engine. Johnny wasn't in sight, and her mind was racing wildly. No time to think as she put the ignition in reverse and stomped on the gas pedal. The wagon lurched backward, and as she came closer to the road, a sudden object struck the windshield. A knife punctured it's way through the glass and stuck there. Startling Wendy as her arm turned the wheel abruptly, sending the wagon back into a telephone booth and striking against the pole that held the diner's neon road sign. The rear window shattered loudly when the metal struck the objects, and the pole came crashing down on the vehicle's top with a thunderous collision. Several of the car's windows broke in fragments, and the roof of the car caved in slightly. It wasn't completely crushed, but the car was now pinned under the road sign indefinitely. Wendy's tears gushed down her face as she saw Johnny standing outside the diner's entrance. He had a look of severe disdain for her and his tentacle arms rose high above his head, threateningly. Wendy put the car in drive, and the rear wheels screeched persistently on the pavement. Wendy cried in fear as the alien-like being began walking toward her. The rubber on the wheels smoked as she strained her foot on the gas. She yelled at the machine to move in fear of her life, banging on the steering wheel and the horn. Cursing every word she could think of until the wagon finally lunched forward. Johnny's eyes grew wide as the car darted toward him slamming into his slimy body and sending him flying over the ground.

Not even bothering to stop, Wendy swerved the car onto the road and headed in the opposite direction she came from. She knew it was too far back to Roswell at this point, and the next town would be closer. The speedometer was reaching ninety as she noticed the fogbank again...this time c̶o̶m̶i̶n̶g̶ from the other side in the direction she was heading. She wasn't going to let up. She didn't care if something was inside. She just needed to get away as fast as she could go. The wagon zoomed through the cloud going over a hundred miles per hour. Wendy could barely see through her own tears as she drove. Her glasses were long gone. Lost somewhere at the Moonbeam Diner. Her life had taken a new turn...a terrifying turn...and she didn't know if it would ever be the same. The clouds of the fog lifted quicker than before, and Wendy's vision was soon met with a large truck coming toward her. The man in the truck gasped at the sight of the wagon hurtling toward him, and he blared his horn. Wendy screamed and yanked the wheel to the right as the car screeched over the road sideways, buckling the wheels and sending the vehicle into a rolling crash. She lost control completely and blacked out as the wagon tore itself apart with every roll until finally resting in a ditch along the highway. The man in truck stopped quickly and ran toward the wrecked wagon laying upside down over two yards away. Steam was rising out of the hood, and he was sure the driver was long dead by now. It was only to his dismay to find the woman still alive and gasping for air as he pulled the door off the hinges. Wendy could barely see. Her vision was obscured by the flows of blood streaming from her head, and she could not move her arms and legs. She couldn't feel anything at all, except the cold. The man dragged her out of the car and carried her back to his truck. She thought she heard him say something about a hospital and to "keep breathing" but she couldn't do anything but lay in his arms. The light faded away again, and her eyes closed softly in the wind.

PART TWO

MR. WHITE

Chapter 5

It crept between the cracks of light with soundless blurs and murmurs. Shadows looming near with gentle motions as they quietly came into focus. The sound of a distant hum floated above, following a breeze across her skin. A ceiling fan spun at low speed as Wendy's eyes awakened. Hushed voices drew louder as the shadows stepped closer. They moved like ghosts around her bed, and Wendy found herself laying still and soft. The shorter figure came close as it spoke, jolting Wendy's memory out of deep slumber state. A woman kneeling by her side, with long black hair and chestnut colored eyes gave a warm smile. Her lips were red in color from the shade of her make-up, and she took Wendy's hand in delicate fashion.

"Hi Wendy" the woman said softly. She recognized this woman to be Christine, her only sibling. Wendy's eyes opened completely now, noticing there was only one other person in the room. A heavy-set man at the foot of the bed with large, round glasses and a long white doctor's coat. He held a clipboard in his hands as he clasped them together in front of himself.

"Chis...tine?" Wendy spoke, turning her head to face her. Her face felt very heavy, as did her own body, and she stopped herself from trying to move. Her sister nodded, and let a few tears trickle down her cheeks.

"Yes, Wendy...it's me" she answered. Her voice sounded distraught and dry, as though she'd been upset for a while now. Wendy's eyes looked at the man below her as he adjusted his glasses. He was now writing something in his notes and casually glancing at the young woman in the bed.

"Where...am I?" she asked them. She attempted to move again, but her body still felt like a rock. She almost didn't recognize the feeling of her own weight.

"Good afternoon, Wendy. I'm Dr. Patterson" the man said finally. His voice was much older than she thought it would be, and he clearly looked younger than he appeared. "You're at St. Mary's hospital in Roswell. Try not to move, you've been in a terrible accident."

Wendy's eyes opened wider as she focused them, noticing two different IV needles in her arms. Christine caressed her sister's cheek and lightly moved Wendy's red hair to the sides. She was still knelt beside the bed, holding back more of her tears. By the way she was staring, Wendy began to feel very cautious. As though these people all knew something that she didn't.

"How long have I been here?" she asked again, her voice becoming clearer now. She swallowed a few times, trying to relieve her dry throat, and Christine brought a glass of water to her lips. Wendy eagerly drank it, feeling it spill down her chin a bit. She realized just how thirsty she truly was. Dr. Patterson took in a breath with a serious face and removed his glasses.

"Miss Fields...this may come as a shock to you, and I'm going to tell you this as gradual as possible. Try not to over-excite yourself" he warned. Wendy lifted her head as Christine held her sister's hand firmly.

"Wendy...it's 1962. You've been unconscious for two years" her sister whispered. The doctor made a sigh when Christine spoke before him and Wendy's heart began to accelerate.

"The accident left you in a coma." The doctor continued, "We were able to stabilize your body and keep you alive, but you suffered serious fractures and internal bleeding. We had to operate to stop your injuries from becoming fatal."

Wendy stared at the man intently without blinking, wide-eyed and surprised. She couldn't believe what she was hearing. This man and her sister literally just told her that two years of her life was now gone, and she could still clearly remember being carried away from her car. The accident was still fresh in her mind, and yet...everything was new...and changed. Her brain was still in 1960...but the world had gone on without her.

Dr. Patterson carefully set down his clipboard on a small nearby table, and began to walk slowly to Wendy's left side of the bed. It was now, a small rainstorm was beginning outside. Trickles of water splashed against the glass of the room's only window on the left side wall, and the light was growing dimmer. It did rain in Roswell, but usually only during the summer months. This gave Wendy a hint at what time of the year it was now. The doctor retained a stern, but thoughtful expression as he held his hands behind his back. Speaking calmly as he walked.

"Miss Fields, the accident you were in left your body in quite a damaged state. Frankly, I'm not sure how you survived it, but I'm glad you did" he told her, seemingly to stare at the wall beside the bed rather than his patient. He seemed hesitant, but he wasn't going to stop speaking now. It was clear that he didn't want to worry the woman any further, given the fact she'd already been through a traumatic ordeal. Wendy blinked gently, waiting for him to continue. She never moved, and she couldn't help but feel a bit impatient now. "As I said before, we were able to stop your internal bleeding, but...your right leg was broken beyond healing state. As a result...we had to amputate it at the knee. Otherwise the possible dangers of bone disease and gangrene were fairly certain" he explained. He seemed overly professional in some fashion, and she couldn't help but feel disrespected by him not turning to face her. He did however, help to save her life, and she was very much grateful to him. Christine couldn't hold her tears at the sound of the doctors words, and was now crying in her hands as she continued to kneel by the bed. Wendy stared blankly down at her feet below her...or now...her foot below her. She noticed how the blanket sank lower on the right side, indicating the loss of her other leg and it began to sink in. Her leg was...*gone*. She still had her thigh, but...her ability to walk was forever gone. She didn't know what to do – what to think – or even say at this point. Her tears made her body jump when she felt them. She didn't even know she was crying too. She just simply stared ahead of herself, remembering all the times she could walk...run...stand up...or dance. These simple, yet forgetful memories flooded her mind so quickly that a wave of dizziness engulfed her. Her breaths heightened and she gasped for air, reaching forward with her arms, but the doctor held her back. He was fast, needing quickly to restrain her before any further injuries could occur. Wendy had spent the last two years in recovery, but her body was still very frail and weak. It would be a while before she could do anything her brain was used to doing before the accident. It was like waking up in another body. Suddenly finding yourself incapable of moving the same way you always did before. A trapping feeling that made her want to scream, but she couldn't. Her voice was too weak, and she only laid there in the man's arms, as her mouth fought for the sound. Dr. Patterson abruptly poked a long syringe within Wendy's skin, and the little amount of strength Wendy had, soon melted away. In her mind she was screaming *"Why me! Why cut my leg off! WHY!"* but the words never surfaced. Her eyes slowly closed and her mind was left to wander.

The doctor successfully calmed her down by sedating her, and Christine held her sister's hand in her own. She'd been told that Wendy may react like this, but she never knew how heart-wrenching it would be to see it happen. All the years of their quarrels and the distance placed between them now weighed heavily on her mind in regret. She wished she had been there more often for her sister in the past, and now she was determined to be here for her as much as she needed.

Chapter 6

The wind felt hot against her face while standing in the rocky sand. The sky, erupting brightly in hues of red and orange against a gloomy background. A shadowy black sky with bursts of fire raging high into the air. Wendy stood alone in the rocky desert, fighting the will to move. Ahead of her...the chromed Moonbeam Diner sat within a hellish landscape. The windows all blackened from the flames that engulfed around them, and the stars completely vanished above the horizon. The ground below it was melting sluggishly as the earth broke apart.

There was no sound. Behind her lay a vast sea of lava as massive volcanic mountains gorged through the crust, making her feel isolated. She couldn't move, nor speak. She simply stared ahead as the door of the diner crept open in silence. It was deafening...at how much the loss of sound weighed heavily on her ears. Just to hear anything would be a relief. A yellowish light pierced into her eyes from the doorway as a pair of gleaming eyes shown there. They preyed upon her with a green vibrancy and she felt her stomach knot inside. She couldn't see herself, and the sight of the ground coming closer to her face gave a sign that she'd fallen to the ground while the creeping figure gazed at her. Long blackish tentacles snaked their way around the figure as they curled along the exterior walls of the diner, slithering in a slimy film as they dripped lightly. A long protruding tongue swerved its way out of the figure's mouth from between its long white fangs, wiggly at her with curious delight. It was black in color, and it oozed with saliva as its green eyes grew wider. Seeming to gain Wendy's scent as hot breaths wafted from its throat. Wendy gave a loud scream as she watched the creature slide its way toward her on the ground, nearly reaching her face as her eyes opened quickly.

Wendy's body was drenched in sweat as Christine came up to her. She had a worrisome expression on her face and she held her sister's hands in comfort. Wendy squeezed them tightly as she began to regain consciousness. She was trying to catch her breath as Dr. Patterson soon followed into the room.

"Are you alright, Miss Fields?" he asked quickly. He seemed genuinely more concerned than the first time she spoke to him, and Wendy shook her head slowly.

"It's...very...hard to...breathe" she whispered loudly. The man placed a stethoscope on Wendy's chest and listened for a few moments. Wendy gradually began to catch her breath again as the doctor looked at her vitals on the monitors behind her.

"You're going to be alright. You had a scare, and your body almost passed out, but your vitals are doing just fine. In fact, you've been getting better everyday, Wendy" he told her with confidence. Wendy slowly made a smile and she closed her eyes, breathing long and deep breaths for her lungs to replenish themselves.

"I...had a terrible nightmare" Wendy admitted. She looked up at the doctor and her sister, and she gently pushed herself further upright in the bed off the pillows. "It was..." she started to say, but she stopped herself. Staring down at her missing limb she began to wonder what the doctor may think of her if she mentioned anything about Johnny and the Moonbeam Diner. She wondered...if the experience even happened at all. It was still so fresh in her memory. The dream was proof of that, and yet…if that was Johnny in her dream…he was even more grotesque than what she remembered. There is something more about him. Something far beyond everyone's understanding. It was a lonely feeling as it swept over her. Who was she going to tell? Who would ever believe that she was attacked by…whatever he was? Some sort of… "…alien." She whispered allowed. Christine stood up from the bed, and backed away slightly. Her eyes narrowed, but not in disgust or anger. It was a curious expression after hearing what her sister had whispered. Dr. Patterson nodded his head, and seemed to disregard most of what Wendy was saying. Possibly dismissing it as a simple nightmare, and one of many she would likely have in the weeks or months to come as a recovering coma victim.

"All is well now, Miss Fields. You're bound to have nightmares after going through such a traumatic event. You needn't worry too much over them, for it's all a part of your recovery process" he told her confidently. "Allow me to see if the kitchen is ready for meals, you'll need to eat to build strength."

Wendy nodded back to the man as he turned away out of the room. Christine sat down in a wooden chair beside the bed, and Wendy watched her staring for nearly a minute before speaking up.

"What?" she asked her. Christine crossed her legs and leaned forward in the chair. She spoke audibly, but just enough for the both of them to hear.

"Who is Johnny?" she asked quietly. Her brown eyes never blinked when she questioned her. Christine was the only person Wendy knew who could be perplexed and serious at the same time. In such a way, that it felt intimidating at times. She acted like she discovered a secret, but she didn't know why or what it was. Wendy was as surprised. She was almost terrified to hear her sister say that name...even though she'd never mentioned him before. Her eyes were slowly widening and she whispered a reply, feeling shaken and cold.

"How...do you know...about him?" she breathed. Christine raised a brow, and leaned closer as she brought her leg down again. She clasped her hands in front of herself casually.

"At night...I would hear you say things" she began, "You were still in a coma at the time, but...you were slowly recovering each day. Slowly regaining consciousness. The doctor said you were only mumbling random words, but you spoke them more than once…several times."

Wendy put a hand over her chest as her breath sped up again, trying to calm herself. It literally felt like someone had caught her doing something terrible, and now she was left to explain herself.

"What would I say?" she asked her. Christine twiddled her fingers as she looked around the room. The doctor still hadn't come back, and she didn't want him to yet. She wanted to talk with Wendy alone, and she hadn't gotten many moments to do so since Wendy woke from being comatose.

"You…only ever said two words. Johnny and moonbeam. I never could figure out why. You would repeat them in interludes of five minutes or less for a few hours, and then stop. As though you were thinking of someone or remembering something. I was always here, helping to watch over you. I haven't been in Phoenix since the night you wrecked your car" she admitted. "I just want to know, Wendy…what exactly happened to you."

A small roll of thunder boomed over the hospital as the rain continued. The storm wasn't letting up, and it made the natural light of the room very dreary without the overhead lamp turned on. Wendy looked very pale in this setting. Almost ghostly, and Christine had never seen her this way before. Whatever had happened to her, it was something that altered the woman's life forever now. Something that would always be there...a part of her soul. Wendy was forever changed.

Swallowing hard and leaning upright in the bed, Wendy set her hands in front of herself contently, as if getting ready to tell a story. She was far from relaxed, but she nearly looked like a dying old grandmother – bedridden and lonely. Her eyes were heavy with dark circles, indicating her lack of proper sleep as of late. Or sleeping too much entirely.

"Christine...do you remember the news story back in the late 40's? The one about the...space ship?" she asked her. Christine held her breath for a moment, but answered calmly.

"You mean...the Roswell Incident?"

Wendy gave a weak nod and she stared at her with glassy eyes. "Yes" she said. Christine's hands felt sweaty and numb in her clasp, and she shook them lightly to get the blood flowing through them again.

Wendy…what are you trying to say…?" she asked her. The red hairs on Wendy's head fell silently against her face, but she kept staring. As though a trance had come over her mind, it was the most serious and worn out expression Christine had ever seen on her sister.

"For a moment…open your mind…and try not to let common logic distract you" Wendy began. "As children…we're allowed to let our minds wander and think about the impossible. To wonder about the things that go bump in the night, and know it's not just the wind…but something more. As children…we know more than adults ever will…because we see the world for how it really is. We don't let responsibility get in the way of our thoughts. All we do is watch…and discover life's secrets around us. Even if those secrets…aren't from this world at all."

Wendy's body wasn't moving. She resembled a doll laying in the blankets, tucked comfortably as a tear strolled down the side of her cheek. She spoke so softly and slow, it began to scare Christine as she listened to her feeble voice.

"Wendy…what did you see?" she questioned delicately. Wendy's eyes were fixed when she replied, and her fear showed through her voice. She was terrified to speak any louder than this.

"I...drove through a fog...but...I don't think it was one" she said.

"What do you mean?" Christine asked.

"This fog...was *different*. It was so cold inside the cloud that...it made my car ice over. I thought I was going to freeze...until..." Wendy stopped.

"Until what?" her sister nudged.

"I saw a light...a blinding blue light glowing through. It was so bright...and the fog drifted away. I remember the stars were so large. They didn't look normal. *Nothing*...looked completely normal. The light was coming from a diner. It was called the Moonbeam Diner...and...it wasn't right. It just didn't *feel* right when I touched it. The door was vibrating when I reached for it. The inside was so clean...it almost didn't seem real. I remember a jukebox...it only played one song. "Sleep Walk." Wendy explained. Christine's curiosity rose over her as she listened.

"And...that's when I met him. *Him.* He said his name was Johnny...and he was gorgeous. So *handsome*. I don't know why...but I *wanted* him. I wanted him as soon as I saw him. He asked me for my order, and then I waited. I remember waiting for a long time before I tried to find him. I went into the kitchen, but...he wasn't there, Christine. I didn't know where he was until..."

"Until...? Her sister asked again. "Wendy...what did you... *see?*" She leaned against the bed, holding her sister's hand closely as Wendy's tears became more frequent. The woman's voice was so shaken and weak, she could only whisper when she spoke.

"There were...*things*...in the basement. It was people, Christine...piles of *people.* They were stacked together on the floor...in *pieces...*" Wendy murmured. Christine brought a hand to her mouth at the sight of her sister's face. So distraught and afraid while trying to share her experience as much as her memory would allow. "He was standing in the back corner...cooking something...and that's when I seen them. His other arms...he wasn't *human...*" Wendy sobbed, covering her face in her hands as Christine reached forward, taking her in her arms and holding her close. Wendy continued to cry as she rambled. Her voice becoming louder now, and breaking in between words. "I tried to get away! I ran as fast as I could and...he almost got me! I barely got to the car in time, and drove away...running him over and going back through the fog! There was a truck on the other side, and I swerved out of the way and rolled so many times!" she cried. Christine held her gently, rocking her body softly as she tried to calm her down again. Dr. Patterson came into the room with a look of concern, and quickly ran over to the bed.

"Miss Fields! Are you alright? What's happened?!" he asked them. Christine spoke up before Wendy could, and immediately laid her sister back down on her pillow.

"She had another nightmare...a bad one. I rushed over to calm her down, but...she's very upset. I think she just needs to cry and get it out...no more drugs. She just needs to breathe!" she said, raising her voice. Dr. Patterson stepped back and observed the two women on the bed in apprehension. He nodded to them agreeably, and walked back to the door, pulling in a wheeled cart with a food plate on top of it.

"You'll need to eat soon, Wendy. Please make the effort to keep your strength, or your recovery will be much longer than you need it to be" he told her. He handed the young woman a damp cloth for her to wipe her face and tears, and placed a hand over her shoulder in comfort. "It's going to get better from now on...I promise you."

Wendy made a small smile, but turned her eyes to the floor as she sat up again. There was a sudden loud knock on the door, and everyone's heads turned to face it. All three of them were surprised, and seemed to ignore it until Dr. Patterson asked who was there. When the door opened, it was slow and creeping. The hinges gave a shriek at the sluggish pace, and a tall man stepped forward into the room. He was dressed formally, in a deep black business-like suit and wearing heavily tinted sunglasses. The light reflected off them in dismal fashion, blocking any sight of eyes as he slowly came toward them. His expression was stern. His hair was short and black - the same shade as his clothing and it almost looked plastic from the use of hair oil. He held his hands behind his back as he stopped by the foot of the bed. Everyone gleaming at him as he stared directly at Wendy in her bed.

"Miss Wendy Fields...I presume" he said to her. His voice was slithery. It rolled off his tongue in a lightened tone. It sounded more cheerful than his terribly stern face, which looked quite angry, but professional. It was odd...but his voice gave the feeling of a childish demeanor. It made them want to chuckle when they heard it, but it was creepy all the same. He remained very stoic where he stood, waiting for an answer as he gradually tilted his head to one side. The action reminded them of a curious cat, without moving his mouth.

"Y-Yes...I am" Wendy replied softly, wiping her face with the cloth. "Who are you?" she asked him. The man brought his head back up right and spoke again in the same odd tone as before.

"You may call me Mr. White" he told her simply. Both Christine and the doctor narrowed their eyes, and Wendy's sister spoke first.

"I don't believe we know you" Christine said, tightening her tone. "What do you want with my sister?"

Mr. White continued to stand where he was, and never moved an inch of his face toward the woman. He stared blankly at Wendy with his shimmering dark spectacles.

"I'm not complied to answer you, Miss Christine Fields. I am here for Wendy only" he said.

"Sir...if you're not family, then I must ask you to leave now. This area is a private recovery ward, and this room is off limits to those unrelated to the patients" the doctor warned. Mr. White's head turned slowly to the man beside him, and he gave a firm answer.

"Dr. Eli Patterson. I work for the government...on a very high level. You will find that I have every right to be in this room, and if you interfere with me any further, I will have you arrested and your licensed revoked" the man said in his sly-like voice. He spoke every word so clearly and precise. He almost seemed unreal. The way he sounded reminded Wendy of a robot in a sci-fi movie. Was he trying to be professional? He only seemed to mimic a false human tone, in a sarcastic manner. The doctor's eyes widened and his voice began to fume.

"*Arrested?!* On what grounds?!" he questioned. Mr. White turned away, staring at Wendy once again, and never moving from his spot.

"On the *grounds* that my superiority is *higher* than yours. Now if you don't mind. I'll ask *you* to leave the room now. You're disrupting my investigation" the man demanded. Staring deeply into the man's dark round sunglasses made Wendy's stomach feel ill. There was a rise of tension and it made her feel afraid. She'd never met this man before, and nor did she know what he wanted with her. There was a heavy silence between them both and she could almost feel a link between them. A vibration in the air and her eyes began to fade with tunnel vision. There was something about this man...something different. *Very* different. Dr. Patterson had left the room, quite hurriedly in fact, and Christine knelt down beside her sister quickly.

"You've seen something that you shouldn't have seen...*haven't* you, Miss Fields?" Mr. White informed. It was an obvious question that she didn't need to answer. Wendy simply nodded slowly, feeling dazed and lost within the man's voice. Like an echo creeping far into her mind as his pasty white face loomed near her.

"You went through the fog...*didn't* you, Wendy?" the man whispered intently. She nodded again, and Christine moved her own body in front of her sister. Three hospital security guards came running into the room with Dr. Patterson following behind. They grabbed Mr. White and pulled backward promptly. The suited man lurched out of their grasp and quickly made his way out of the room in a speedy fashion.

"No need for that gentleman! I've heard all that I needed to hear!" he shouted out. Which was clearly nothing. Wendy hadn't said a thing, and yet Mr. White acted like she did. The security men followed Mr. White out of the room to escort him to the parking lot. "We shall meet again, Miss Fields. Very soon indeed" he called to her from down the hall. A door slammed harshly in the distance and one security officer came back to the room.

"We're very sorry you had to deal with that. He must've been a reporter or something" he said. Dr. Patterson took a deep breath and nodded, wiping his forehead with a handkerchief.

"I want you men standing guard of this room until Miss Fields is ready for discharge" he told them. His voice was much harder than before, clearly angry with the fact that someone unrelated and possibly threatening came so close to his patient. Wendy surprised everyone by speaking, since the last several minutes she seemed to be in a trance-like state.

"Why would reporters want to see me?" she asked softly. The doctor sighed, and sat himself down on the end of the bed.

"You've been out for a long time, Wendy. People had wondered where you went. Your employer, Walter Johnson called a police investigation out for you, but you were quickly brought here by a passing trucker after you crashed your wagon. He told us how you almost hit him coming out of a fogbank" he explained. Christine stroked her sister's hair once again, attempting to keep Wendy relaxed.

"I came here as soon as I heard what happened. I drove the whole way from Phoenix, and I've been here ever since. Jack had to bring me clothes from home since I left in a hurry" she admitted. Looking at her sister and hearing these words nearly made Wendy cry as she listened. She reached up and gave an embrace as she whispered.

"I'm glad you're here, Christine. I...don't want to be alone" she told her.

"I know...and I'm going take care of you. You will get better, Wendy, I promise" Christine said gently. The feel of Wendy's fingers gripping tightly on her sister's arms was enough assurance to know how much she was needed now. Christine was the only family Wendy had left in this world. She didn't want to lose another person in her life. Or worst of all...her *own* life.

The wind outside the window gave a low groan, and some dust from the ground hit the glass. Wendy swallowed hard again, finding it difficult to keep her throat lubricated. Without even asking, Christine brought another glass of water with a straw up to Wendy's lips.

"You're going to feel thirsty for a few days most likely" Dr. Patterson informed. "It's one of the after affects from the feeding tube we gave you while your body was comatose."

Wendy gave a slow nod, listening to her doctor as she sipped. She could feel her strength returning little by little, and she only felt pain when the morphine began to wear off.

"I've got to say, Miss Fields...you're a very lucky patient. Most coma victims don't recover after such long periods of unconsciousness. And given the fact your body seems to have responded very well upon waking up. I removed your feeding tube an hour before you woke, when your body was showing clearer signs of recovery. You seemed to have been in a dream-like state for a long time, even speaking in your sleep...but never fully reviving until now. I'm not even sure if I'd call your case completely comatose. However, it was the only conclusion I came to upon observing your condition. You may very well be the first person to ever be in a half-state coma and fully awake two years later" the doctor mentioned. His voice was calmer now, more focused and alert. Wendy had been staring at him with large eyes, and listening closely. She tried to make sense of it, but she could tell that he was very confused about her sudden recuperation. It surprised her as well...for she now knew, she was two years older. Being age thirty-one currently, and feeling as though she was lost in the Twilight Zone. It made her stomach queasy just thinking and wondering how much of her life she had missed. What would everyone be doing now? Was her home okay? Who had taken care of her bills and payments? What became of her car? Had she lost her job as Walter Johnson's secretary? And most of all...the creeping loom of darkness in her mind...the figure of Johnny standing in the doorway of his chromed Moonbeam Diner. *What...*had become of *him.* Should she tell anyone else? And who was the mysterious Mr. White? She could still see his dark sunglasses peering down at her from above. Like a ghost etching in her mind...he loomed there. Something about him wasn't right. He seemed abnormal and oddly giddy. Maybe that wasn't the right word for him, but he was surely impatient about something that had to do with her....and the biggest question of all, was how he knew about her trip through the fog. He knew something that she didn't, and his presence wasn't going away anytime soon. She was sure of that.

"Am I...ever going to walk again?" Wendy asked, staring down at her lonely leg under the blankets of her bed. Dr. Patterson bit his lower lip as he watched a small tear trickle down the woman's cheek. This was the part of his profession that kept him awake at night. Having to tell people how their lives have changed forever. Sometimes, it was positive...and other times it wasn't. *This*...was one of those times when it wasn't.

"No, Wendy...I'm afraid not" he told her, gently placing a hand on her leg. She moved it back slightly, and he quickly pulled his hand back to himself again, knowing she didn't want to be comforted. "However..." the doctor continued, and Wendy raised her eyes at him, "You may consider the use of a prosthetic limb. After operating, I'm quite sure your leg will heal just fine now. I have no doubt you could use a prosthetic leg to help your balance...and be able to walk again."

Wendy's eyes lightened at the thought of possible hope shining over her situation. Christine stood up again, folding her arms and spoke up.

"Aren't those fake legs unreliable? I've heard stories of old war men from the '40's having to use them. They're apparently not very comfortable" she said. She held doubt in her tone, but she was also curious about this new information. She was wanting it to be a positive turn of events. Dr. Patterson shook his head, and stood up as well, placing his hands in his white coat pockets.

"On the contrary, the medical field has advanced them in the last decade. They're quite reliable, and safe to use. Wendy would have to learn to walk with it, and I'll personally teach how to do so. I've helped many of those men from wartime you mentioned. All of them are alive today and still using their... *fake legs*" he enlightened. "And not just legs, but arms and hands as well."

"I would like to try it..." Wendy spoke up, shifting her eyes between her sister and the doctor. They were welling with tears, and her voice was shaken, but she was determined not to live the remainder of her life in a bed. "I...don't want to live...without walking" she told them. She wiped a few of her tears away in a long frown, and took a breath. Looking up at them again, she nodded in agreement. "I'm willing to do this."

"You will have weeks to months of physical therapy, Wendy. Not just for coma recovery, but also for your mobility. We will need to be sure you can walk on your own before you live alone again. Christine took Wendy's hands into her own and nodded to the doctor.

"She won't have to be alone, since I'll be staying with her for a while. She'll need me there with her. I've already arranged to stay in Roswell for as long as she needs me to" she announced. Wendy's emotion leaped up through her chest at the sound of her sister wanting to help her to literally find her feet again. For the first time since waking up...she felt a reason to smile, even if it was small and weak. She was glad she wouldn't be alone. After everything that had happened, the thought of being alone in her home was a harrowing feeling. Wendy felt very vulnerable now, and she needed someone she could trust to be with her. It was also for the first time, in a long time...she saw the light inside Christine. After several years apart, it was heartfelt that she was willing to be here. Their mother would be overjoyed if she were still alive. What brought out this change in Christine, Wendy wasn't sure completely, but maybe just the thought of her younger sister nearly dying in a car accident was enough to snap Christine back to reality. The reality that someone else's life was more important than her own selfish needs.

Chapter 7

Stepping out through the door into the small courtyard of hospital, Wendy's blue eyes looked up at the sky as the sun shone brightly above. Fluffs of clouds drifted far ahead in silence, and the heat of a warm breeze blew softly on Wendy's face like an old friend. A small flowerbed of irises swayed in the wind as Wendy took in the world around herself once again. It had been a while…a long, long while. For her, it didn't feel all that long ago, but in reality she hadn't been outside the hospital in two years, and her body was taking in a deep breath of freshness. Live was welcoming her back again, and she slowly felt a smile form over her lips. The crutches that held her in place were now very familiar to her. She'd been practicing walking with her new leg for over a month now. Christine and Dr. Patterson stood behind her as she carefully made her way to a nearby bench to rest. Hobbling around was normal for her, but she was getting the hang of walking almost normally again. Soon, she probably wouldn't need the crutches anymore, but the doctor encouraged her to use them for added support. It was certainly better than having to spend her life in a wheelchair.

"How do you feel?" Dr. Patterson spoke up, sitting down on the bench beside her. Wendy gazed up at the tree in the center of the small courtyard and watched the lush greenness of the leaves dance with trickles of sunlight. They moved together in quiet harmony.

"I missed this..." she whispered, gently wiping a tiny teardrop from her cheek. She felt Christine's hand holding her own and she smiled at them both. "I missed being outside" she told them softly. Dr. Patterson removed his glasses and placed a hand on his patient's shoulder. He was proud of his accomplishment – proud of helping Wendy not only to walk again, but giving her life back to her. Seeing how quickly she recovered from a coma had amazed him.

"I think it's time you rejoined the world, Wendy" he told her.

Turning the brass doorknob of her front door, Wendy was soon greeted by a settled aroma of old wood furniture and dust when she stepped into her living room. It had been a long while since she'd been here...even if her memories told her differently. They told her she had been gone only one night, even if by now she had spent close to two months in the hospital recovering after two years of coma. She still felt as though she left on her drive to Phoenix and suddenly appeared at home. It was strange to be here again. Although it felt familiar...it was like walking into a dream. Like a place long forgotten from her past. Everything was right where it was before she left, but covered in dust surrounded by warm stale air. It reminded her of coming home from a long vacation...but one she could not remember. She lingered in the doorway with her sister standing behind her. Her legs didn't seem to want to move now, and her mind was just so lost and confused. Feeling a gentle nudge from behind, Christine helped Wendy walk into her home again. Wendy blinked her eyes while stepping forward, and the action was automatic. Christine walked around her in the living room and set their purses down on the coffee table nearby. Their mother's portrait still sat up on the mantle by a clock long silent from the gears running down. It would have to be wound again, Wendy thought to herself. She was looking around the room at everything she'd have to do in order to make herself familiar again. Odd enough, she had to practice doing everyday things even if her mind remembered how to them. She no longer had much trouble moving around or lifting things, but her walking cane certainly helped her balance.

"I kept track of all your bills" Christine spoke up, holding her hands in front of herself comfortably. She looked as though she was presenting the house as a realtor. "I dusted as often as I could, but I didn't get to clean everything" she admitted. Wendy took a sigh as she stared up at the ceiling and she turned her head to Christine.

"It's fine. Thank you for keeping the house safe for me. We'll start cleaning tomorrow" she said calmly. Christine smiled and began walking to the kitchen.

"I stocked the fridge with new food. I'll make us some dinner" she announced. Wendy smiled in return and slowly sat herself down on the couch to rest.

"Sounds good" she replied.

A pot of macaroni and cheese with fried canned spam is what their dinner consisted of for the night. Christine, not particularly being well trained in cooking, had made the meal and the two sisters sat quietly in Wendy's small dining room. A mahogany wood grandfather clock stood behind Christine to the back corner of the room by a small window, where it swayed it's pendulum in low ticks in the otherwise silent setting. A brass candelabrum was lit between them on the table, even though the chandelier above was more than enough light. Christine was watching Wendy stare down at the plate of food, and made a soft sigh.

"I guess my cooking skills haven't improved over the years. You were always the better chef that me" she admitted, breaking the silence. Wendy blinked and looked up at her sister, whom now had a sullen expression on her pale face behind her make-up. Seeing her sister look like this, made Wendy realize that Christine was trying her best to make Wendy feel more at home again. She made a kind smile, and took a bite of spam. To her surprise, it wasn't bad at all, and she was rather enjoying it.

"No, no...I was just...lost in my thoughts" Wendy replied. "The food's good. You did well, sis" she commented. Christine became more delighted, and handed Wendy the salt and pepper shakers.

"I bought a lemon torte for dessert too. I remember when Mom used to make them, and the whole house would smell sweet. I know I *definitely* wouldn't be able to make one like she did, so I stopped by the shops to get it" she announced. Wendy took a long drink of her ice water and then made a sudden change of subject that caught her sister by surprise. So much so, that she wondered why she chose such a personal question that had nothing to do with their current conversation.

"What happened with you and Jack?" she asked, interrupting Christine's talk of lemon tortes. Wendy eyes were focused on the plate below her, cutting pieces of spam into smaller ones and eating casually after questioning. Christine was staring at her sister in confusion, and soon set her fork down. She looked off the side of the room and held her own ice water between her hands without drinking it yet.

"Well...as you've probably guessed, we never got married" she admitted, almost reluctantly. Wendy took off her new pair of cat's eye glasses and set them on the table. She folded her arms and gave Christine her full attention.

"How come?" she asked again. Christine took a drink and shrugged her shoulders.

"I learned that it wasn't meant to be. He wasn't husband material" she said. Wendy began to nod her head in agreement as she listened to these words. "And besides, he wasn't very keen on the fact that I literally dropped everything and drove to here to Roswell the day I heard about your accident."

Now intrigued, Wendy raised a brow and leaned forward slightly in her chair. She noticed Christine's serious eyes looking back at her, knowing she had approached a sore subject.

"What did he say to you?" she asked in a more genial tone. Christine made a long sigh, but not from annoyance. She seemed rather lost and confused about her life now. Realizing that everything had taken a dramatic turn for the both of them, and now they were all each other had in the world. Just like when their mother had died. Christine's voice had a melancholy tone when she spoke. She sounded as though she were about to cry, and needed to.

"He...didn't want me to leave. He said your accident wasn't important enough to just leave without warning" she said, setting the glass down on the table again. She brought a hand up to her lips, holding back a few trembling tears that trickled lightly on her cheeks. Wendy slowly reached her arms across the table, and softly took her sister's arm in her hands. "He wanted our Honeymoon to be a trip to the World's Fair in Seattle...which is probably where he is now. He said if I left, then I would never see him again, so...I haven't" Christine announced. She placed her hand over her eyes, and her lips formed a saddened frown as she shuddered. Wendy hadn't known how much her sister loved Jack, and he apparently never felt exactly the same way. She got the vibe from Christine, that he was very controlling over her, and very selfish. Even though the two siblings had fought for years after their mother's death, and never could quite get along, it was Wendy's recent tragedy that brought Christine back home again. Back to the town she originally left behind for a new life.

Wendy made a gentle squeeze on her sister's arm, and Christine opened her eyes again. She left out a quick breath and lifted her head up with mascara running from her eyes.

"Well..." she said through her breaths, "...he was stupid. Just a stupid fuckin' man" she declared, forcing a smile and a small chuckle. Wendy couldn't help but make a smile of her own, but she hardly though the situation was funny. She merely reciprocated Christine's thought to "laugh it off". She was always like that. Christine rarely showed her emotions, and if she did, she was quick to laugh it off again. Burying it deep inside to let it out later when she was alone.

"I'm sorry, Christine..." Wendy said softly. Her sister merely shrugged her shoulders again, lightly moving her arm out of Wendy's grip and made a shooing gesture with her hands.

"Ah, don't be" she replied. "It's over and done with. I've moved back to Roswell anyway. Phoenix wasn't for me" she said, pushing the issue aside. Wendy sighed, and brought her arms together again. She thought of eating more of her food again, but realized it was probably going cold now. Her appetite was fading anyway, so she gave up on finishing her plate.

"Where are you living now, if you moved back here?" she questioned. Christine dried her eyes with a napkin, attempting to wipe away the smeared make-up on her face.

"Jack kept the house in Phoenix. It was *his* anyway...and I packed my things and brought them here. They're in the spare bedroom, where Mom used to sleep. I stayed in a hotel for a little while, but now I'm living here with you" she said. Wendy was surprised to hear this as well, since she hadn't planned for her sister to move back home with her, but without starting a fight over independence, she remembered that her sister honestly had nowhere else to go. She also accepted the fact that she would more than likely need Christine's assistance on her new living situation and recovery. All in all, Wendy was welcome to the idea of having someone around again. They both needed each other right now, and to put their past differences behind them.

"I guess it's just the two of us now" Wendy said, gathering the plates on the table together into one pile. Christine looked up in surprise.

"You mean...you're not upset at the idea of me being here?" she asked her. "I know it was very sudden, but..."

"Don't worry about it. I'm not upset" Wendy interrupted calmly. "It'll be nice having you around here again....and helping me...*walk* again" she admitted. Christine's face held a certain happiness over it that Wendy hadn't seen for many years.

"I promise to be here for you as much as I can" Christine announced. She was warm with relief now, and Wendy could see it. She too, felt much more relieved now that her sister was back home again, and not living a life she would surely regret if she'd stayed in Phoenix. More importantly, knowing she had someone here that cared about her again. Wendy had been more alone than she thought, and knew it more now that her own family was here again. It was the first sign of light at the end of her long, dark tunnel. For a time, she seemed to almost forget about her terrifying experience...and *Johnny* of the Moonbeam Diner. This short contentment would be temporary, however, for the feeling of his existence still lurked in the back of her mind. She'd been thinking of him ever since she left the hospital. Wondering...if he'd truly been killed the day she struck him with her car. Wondering...if he might still be alive.

Chapter 8

Clearing the dust particles off her phonograph in the living room, Wendy was busy getting her home back in order again. Slowly, but surely making everything look the way it did before she left. It felt being in someone else's home, but one that looked much like her own. Christine had dusted now and then when Wendy was being hospitalized, but admitted to not get around to doing it every day. Wendy would never let her home gather this much dust. The thought of her belongings being so unclean was disturbing her, but given the situation of her sister being there to help her, she held back some of her displeasure. Right now, Christine was busy washing dishes in the kitchen and Wendy had hobbled herself into her living room to relax. She was getting better with using the crutches, and rarely needed two of them. Just one was enough for her to get around. She remembered countless times when Dr. Patterson told her it would be easier to walk as time went on.

"It's just like learning any other skill. It takes practice." He had told her. Yeah...practice after falling several times in her hospital room for days. She was passed all that now. So little as humans do we think about everyday common things such as standing and walking...until it's taken away from us.

Rummaging through her stacks of vinyl records, she checked each one for dust and concurred they were still clean enough for playing. It'd been a while since her ears heard some music. On the way home from the hospital she heard some new hit tunes from Connie Francis and Elvis Presley on the radio of Christine's bright red and white Nash Metropolitan. Such a tiny car it was, but *"economical"* is what her sister called it. A step into the future. It reminded Wendy of the Volkswagen Beetle from Germany, but not as smooth looking. Those cars were becoming more popular in American now too. Christine was all about embracing new technology and fashion trends. Since the last time she'd seen her, Christine had adopted the "MOD" look. It was a style starting to gain popularity in Europe currently, especially in London, England. They also started calling it the "Space Age" look. Bright colors and knee high go-go boots made up most of Christine's wardrobe now. She had to go out of town just to get them. She previously mentioned how she'd brought them Phoenix. This earned many stares from the public eye, but Christine was always confident in herself. Maybe in Phoenix, the public would be more forward thinking, but the style was considered very *bold* for the quiet town of Roswell. It was becoming popular among the youth, but Wendy was still quite happy with her polka-dot dresses. Her yellow and white dress was now gone, after being ruined in the crash, but Christine promised to take her shopping for new clothes soon.

    Toward the back of her record stacks sat the 78s. Most of them her mother's old collection, but they now belonged to her. Wendy had been smiling while she cleaned and looked for music to play, it always helped to calm her thoughts. Her smile slowly faded when seen the name *"Johnny"* pop up behind one of the shellacs. It was a recording of Peggy Lee's *"Johnny Guitar"* that her mother bought back in '54 when she saw the movie. Slowly lifting it out of the stack, Wendy began to run her finger over the label silently as he mind began to drift. She was remembering him...*Johnny.* The smell of the Moonbeam Diner started to creep around the air of the room when the needle of the gramophone hit the grooves. The tranquil melody and Peggy's soothing voice seemed to hypnotize as Wendy listened. It was genial...with a magical feeling. Wendy sank to the floor, sitting awkwardly like a child when the song filled the room. A delicate breeze from the evening desert air blew around his face from an open window nearby. She saw his face...his perfect blue eyes and wavy blonde hair as he smiled. His arms around her now as he laid her back upon the floor. He eyes closed while her body fell limp. Wendy couldn't seem to move...and Johnny was in control. The light of the sky grew a deep reddish hue and room began to twist and turn. Her head swam in a dizzying feeling as her eyes shot open from a sudden intrusion. The stark coldness from Johnny's long wet tongue was sliding up her stomach and poking into her belly button. Wendy looked down at him and quickly started shivering as she watched his long sharp teeth tickle her soft skin. His voice crept in a nightmarish tone as he spoke, and his eyes a piercing yellow as his skin melted around his skull into a blackish substance. It was hot when it touched her body, running aimlessly down her sides like the wax of a candle.

"You taste good..." his voice whispered darkly, staring up at her with full intent. His pupils glowing silver as she screamed loudly into the darkness. Her body was jolted awake by Christine's arms as she shook her. Staring up at her sister from the floor, she realized she'd been in some sort of trance when the music was playing. The needle on the gramophone was now stopped at the end of the song, running over the same groove continuously. Christine stopped the record and knelt down beside her sister again.

"What happened?! You were screaming in here! I nearly fell trying to run to you!" she exclaimed. Christine's hands were still wet and soapy from washing dishes. She had on only one shoe, since the other fell off when she ran into the living room. Wendy's shivers were beginning to cease now as she caught her breath, and ran her fingers over her stomach to check for any differences. She could still feel the chilling sensation of Johnny's tongue on her skin, even after waking up.

"It...It was him again" Wendy stuttered. She brought her hands up to her eyes, wiping tears away as they formed. The streams were coming faster than she could wipe them.

"Who?" Christine asked, helping her sister to stand again. Wendy placed a hand over her chest to calm her heartbeat and swallowed hard in her throat.

"J-Johnny..." she managed to say. "It was Johnny...from the diner."

At first, Christine didn't know what she meant until she remembered what Wendy told her about a man named Johnny whom she met at a diner called "Moonbeam" the night before she wrecked her station wagon. Clearly, whatever had happened to Wendy before the accident was still having an effect on her, and it wasn't just something her mind fabricated while comatose. Christine started walking her sister to her bedroom immediately.

"Come on, let's get you to bed. We're going to see Dr. Patterson first thing tomorrow" she told her. Wendy, willing going to her bedroom without hesitation, replied with a quiet tone.

"He won't believe me. No one ever does" she said. Christine sighed, and stood in front of her.

"I...believe you" she admitted.

"You…do?" Wendy asked, looking up from the bed. Christine then nodded to her sister, and wiped her hands on her apron to dry them.

"Yes…I do. Something is going on, and we're going to find out what it is. And whoever Johnny is too."

The morning sun came hot as it loomed over the desert town sky. Not many places in the country have nearly ninety degrees by ten o'clock before noon, but in Roswell the heat could be unpredictable some days. A small air conditioner cooled the living room of Wendy's tiny bungalow styled home. She could hear the distant hum of the machine from where she sat in the kitchen. Even though she only had one of them, it cooled the house significantly when all the doors were left open inside the rooms. Sitting at the kitchen white table while Christine managed some fried eggs on the stove, Wendy gazed lazily at her warped reflection in the percolator beside her. She'd eaten her breakfast already, even though she wasn't hungry, but she remembered it was something she had to force herself to do little by little after coming back home from the hospital. Her body needed to regain its full strength and potential again. It was closer than before, but she still had trouble walking on her new leg.

"What if he thinks I'm crazy..." Wendy mumbled, not making it sound like a question. Her sister turned from the stove without moving her full body and looked at Wendy staring blankly at the silver coffee pot. Her eyes slowly looked up at her without a change of expression. "What if he...locks me away?"

Christine set down the spatula she'd been holding and set the stove knob lower so her eggs wouldn't burn. She stood beside the table with a hand on her hip as she replied quietly.

"He's not gonna do that, Wendy" she said, somewhat sternly but not with anger. Her eyes were serious and her bright red lipstick reflected in the sun from the kitchen window.

"Why not? It's a crazy thing to believe" Wendy said then, sitting motionless. She was so still, that she could easily be a saddened statue in the chair. Only one that lived and breathed. Christine sighed, brushed her hands on her apron and then poured her sister a cup of coffee from the percolator.

"Because *I* believe you. At least...I believe what you're going through is real. And I wanna know who this Johnny really is. Whether he's a part of dreams...or someone you met for real." she admitted. "I won't let Dr. Patterson simply send you to the loon house without explanation."

Wendy swallowed her breath and picked up the coffee with a shaken hand. Her sister reached over and steadied the cup with aide until Wendy had its grip.

"I hope so" Wendy replied delicately. Christine nodded, and turned back to the stove to collect her meal. "We'll be leaving here by noon, so just relax" she told her. "It's only a follow up visit."

Chapter 9

The vinyl leather seats in Christine's little red and white Nash Metropolitan had become quite hot before leaving the house, but the air conditioning felt nice on Wendy's skin. She remembered how hot her wagon used to get during the summer, while only having the windows for air. Having this thought in mind, she began to wonder if she'd ever consider driving again. With her leg now missing and occupied by a fake one, the hope for it seemed minimal. Sometimes she thought about driving, but then an overwhelming feeling of anxiety would sweep over her body and begin to drown her in apprehension of being in another wreck. When she had rolled her station wagon after being chased by Johnny away from the diner, it'd been the first car accident she'd ever experienced. It would be one occurrence she'd never forget.

"Are you alright?" Christine asked, her voice breaking through Wendy's thoughts. Wendy turned to her sister from the window and nodded lightly.

"Yeah. Can I put on some music?" she answered with her own question. She was already reaching for the radio knob before Christine could reply. The sound of Annette Funicello's kid-like voice filled the speakers as she sang about how every night is a date night in Hawaii. The song was thankfully calming as the sisters rode down the avenue nearing into town. Wendy even felt herself bobbing her head to song's beats until it was suddenly interrupted and cut-off by a blaring news bulletin. A man's voice came over the speaker in a hurry, explaining the recent incident of how the town's famed Dr. Eli Patterson was found dead in his car, wrecked against a telephone pole on the main road leading toward the hospital about an hour prior to the news. The information was still a bit sketchy and more details would be coming in later as the media would be informed. He had apparently hit the pole at considerable high speed and the police were still investigating the actual cause of the man's death. It was apparent to be the accident itself that killed the man. Wendy's hands slowly made their way up to her mouth in shock of hearing the news. At first, she couldn't speak. It was all too surprising.

"Oh my god...we're on the same road where it happened" Christine said then. She was staring down the avenue at a line of cars slowly building up as a single officer was busy directing traffic alone around a closed off scene. He looked very preoccupied and stressed as people tried to view the scene of the doctor's tan colored Cadillac wrapped around the pole.

"Look!" Wendy gasped, pointing toward the scene as they came upon it. The front end of Dr. Patterson's Eldorado was caved in terribly, and the telephone pole was leaning slightly to one side. The windshield was shattered and retained a blood-splattered surface from where the man had apparently struck it with his head during the collision.

"Oh how awful…" Christine whispered, bringing the car to a stop. She too, brought her hands up to her lips and stared indefinitely at the tragic scene. The siren lights of an ambulance wagon were rotating red and white flashes on their windows nearby. The pulsing flash made Wendy's eyes blink each time they shined. Since the hospital was merely straight down the road, the response time had been quick, but unfortunately too late to save the man's life. Christine and Wendy watched as several men carried the doctor's body out to the ambulance on a stretcher covered by a long white sheet to protect viewer's eyes from the sight of his mangled body. The paramedics seemed to be in no hurry to do this, indicating the man was indeed deceased. Two more policemen rushed over to quickly hide the scene, but too many people were nearby. Everyone could see what was happening. Including several reporters for the local news lining up by the scene. News had happened in Roswell of course, but when the death of a well-known doctor to the town's history occurred, it was a sudden and notable event.

    Wendy felt a small tear beginning to roll down the side of cheek as she watched the man's lifeless corpse being hauled away. She recalled the days of when the man helped her to regain her sanity and her ability to walk again after her traumatic ordeal. It was already overwhelming to know that one of the few people who helped save her life, was now gone and could no longer aide her in full recovery. Christine could somehow sense this in her sister, and she took Wendy by the handle silently in the car as they watched the ambulance drive away.

"It's gonna be alright, Wendy...I'm here with you" she told her delicately. Wendy closed her eyes, allowing some tears to finally fall from her lashes and take in a long breath. Christine rolled down her car window and began speaking to a man standing near their car whom also been watching the scene.

"Did they say what caused him to wreck his car?" she asked him. The man leaned toward Christine's window as the policemen continued to divert traffic around the damaged Cadillac.

"He apparently suffered a heart attack and then struck the pole...but they're not completely sure yet" the man informed. Christine nodded her head, and thanked the man before rolling her window back up again. The policeman motioned for Christine to drive forward, and she then she did. Wendy's eyes were suddenly locked on a figured standing off to the side of the road as they rode passed the scene. He was dressed all in black, a formal business suit, and a hat to match. He stood in silence with his hands clasped in front of himself as he gazed at them through his dark round sunglasses. He stood beside a long black colored 1960 Edsel as appeared quite interested in the two women going by. Wendy felt a sense of dread as she watched the mysterious man's head seem to turn slowly along with them as they rode by.

"Christine..._look_...it's that man again" she whispered quickly. Christine noticed Wendy pointing out her passenger window at the dark figure looming by the sidewalk. She immediately remembered him as Mr. White from the day at the hospital when Wendy first woke from her coma.

"What is _he_ doing here..." she replied, watching the man's head turn almost completely around as she drove passed him. His body soon followed his head, observing them intently from down the street. Christine could still see him watching from the rear view mirror. She sped up the car and turned down a side street, heading back toward the downtown area.

"Let's go home...I don't feel very safe right now" Wendy admitted, beginning to panic. Christine clutched the steering wheel and focused on the black Edsel car that was now following them from behind at a considerable distance. It wasn't going very fast, but it was stalking them down every street they took. The radio was now busy playing another song, as they hadn't turned it off before. Linda Scott now sang about counting every star as her bold, yet elegant voice carried out inside the vehicle. A slow song drifting around them as they watched the Edsel loom closer from behind. Christine applied more pressure to the gas pedal and tried to go faster down the street, but another car was ahead of them. It lazily drove along and prevented Christine from going any further. Mr. White's menacing round sunglasses could now be seen from his windshield, and reflected the light of the sun in such a way that they looked like large yellow pupils piercing through the dark lenses. His face was stern and motionlessness as he pressed forward. He seemed determined to follow them...and possibly speak to them. Maybe even stop them from reaching the safety of their home. Both Wendy and Christine felt a confrontation would ensue if this mysterious man were to stop them.

"Christine..." Wendy mumbled in a worrisome tone, staring back through the rear window of the car. She squeezed her sister's arm as the black car behind drew nearer. Christine made the last minute decision to whip the small Nash around the car that was ahead of them and slam the gas pedal to the floor. The little car lurched forward as they reached nearly fifty miles per hour speeding down the street. Mr. White kept up behind them, speeding closer than before. Christine knew the police station was just up ahead, and that was where she was going. She blew the horn repeatedly as the little car slid into the parking lot in front of the station. A policeman who'd been standing out front of the building immediately ran over to the panic-stricken women who bolted out of the car.

"Help us! He's following us!" Wendy screamed as she hobbled over to the officer. Christine was frantically trying to steady her sister, who was by now, nearly falling to the ground. She was trying to run, but her new leg couldn't do this.

"Wendy, stop running! You'll hurt yourself!" Christine exclaimed. Wendy ignored her sister and she fell forward into the policeman's arms. She was shaking out of fear as the black Edsel quickly drove by the station.

"That's him!" Wendy shouted, pointing at the car in mad state. The man observed the car turn off down a side street and he helped the young woman to stand again.

"Come inside the station and tell me what happened" she said to them, keeping a clam voice so the women wouldn't feel so threatened. Both Wendy and Christine followed the man inside, now feeling safer since Mr. White left the area. Wendy wasted no time in explaining about how the man seemed to be following them in a stalking manner, and about the first encounter with him at the hospital. She told him everything that had happened up to this point, and he thankfully listened with full attention and keen interest. It seemed to the three of them, that the mysterious Mr. White was trying to avoid unwanted attention, and only wanted to approach the women alone. The policeman suggested they go right home, and he would follow them there for added safety. He would then put a warning out to his fellow officers for the black Edsel and to keep a look out for any further activity that deemed mischievous. At this point, it was the best approach they could do until Mr. White would show himself again. The man, himself, had very little detail about him, and no record of living in the town of Roswell. He was clearly an outsider who'd been staying in the town for quite some time. The officer informed the sisters that he would lead a quiet investigation at the local hotels and motels to see if such a man had been staying there as well. If he found any further information, he would then bring it to their attention. For now, it was the best thing they could do.

Chapter 10

Wendy stared ahead at the glove box of the car as Christine pulled into the driveway of their small bungalow home. She'd been quiet the whole trip back home, not saying a word and staying lost within her thoughts. The policeman that followed them home parked his cruiser on the street and walked over to their car. Some rainclouds gathered above the area and were now dripping a few drops here and there above them. It would be a warm rain, due to the temperature being so hot outside. Wendy's eyes looked up as she seen the water trickle down the windshield. By now the policeman was standing next to the little Nash and talking with Christine about staying safe and only leaving the house for necessities. Their voices began to blur together into one boring drone and Wendy felt alone. She knew she wasn't alone, but...her world was different now. It changed while she was gone. While she slept indefinitely in a coma, unable to move or tell everyone what she experienced. Life was strange all around her and it moved at such a slow, yet rapid state. It was hard to describe to anyone. All she could do was feel the difference. It was like trying to convey a feeling in another language that no one could understand. Or, speak in *their* language that *she* could no longer understand. When Wendy woke up…she felt as though she'd stepped onto another planet. It looked the same, in various ways…but it certainly didn't feel the same. Maybe she never truly woke from her coma…and she was only sleepwalking. Maybe this was all a dream. Just a long and lucid dream that felt too real to be true. Her mind was playing tricks on her…but Wendy wasn't in the mood to laugh. Reality was becoming a creepy thing suddenly, and Wendy was no longer comfortable in her own skin. Was she really here? Sometimes she wondered about it. Wondering if…everything was a big façade.

Christine shook her sister's body until Wendy's eyes focused. The policeman had long left, and Wendy had been locked in a strange trance for the last five minutes.

"What's wrong?" she asked her sister. Christine's eyes were wide as she gazed at her sibling. The rain was pouring now and the windshield was completely washed over with streams of water turning the view of the world into a surrealist painting.

"You weren't responding to me. I tried saying your name six times now…and all you did was stare out the window" Christine informed. She was holding Wendy's hands together and starting to rub them softly. "Your skin is so cold…"

"Sorry…I was…I dunno…" Wendy replied, bringing a hand up to her forehead. "Everything suddenly felt…fake or something" she admitted. "I don't know what was happening."

Christine brushed Wendy's hair way from her eyes, and opened the car door. The sound of the rain was instantly louder.

"Come on…let's go inside. I think you've seen enough for one day" she told her sister. Wendy followed without hesitation and got out of the car without Christine helping her. The rain was a cold reminder that her life was still real, and it felt nice on her skin. Christine offered an umbrella, but Wendy refused. She wanted to feel reality on her skin. She hobbled over to the doorway with Christine close behind. Reaching for the doorknob, she thought distantly to herself in a row of flashbacks that happened throughout the day, and up to this point.

This...this is my life now...this weird and twisted life that keeps getting creepier each day.

Johnny...are you trying to find me?

You better stay away...

You stay away from me.

I don't belong to you.

The memory of him and his threatening eyes pierced deep into her thoughts. It made her loose her balance and fall against the door as she opened it. Thankfully, being caught in Christine's arms close behind her. Wendy didn't say anything. She instead pressed forward and made her way to the living room couch, no matter how many times she may fall to get there. She didn't know if it was a form of courage or determination, but she wasn't going to let the thought of Johnny stop her from doing simple things like trying to walk again. A part of her, as scared and uncertain as she was, knew she'd been letting those monstrous thoughts dominate her mind. She would do her best not to let them stop her from now on.

When the evening hours drifted closer, the desert sky loomed overhead with a luminous orange glow as the white cirrus clouds rolled high in the atmosphere. It was a gorgeous sunset and it reflected gently in Wendy's eyes as she watched it from her back porch. She occasionally would sit out there on pleasant days when the twilight faded softly in the horizon. It was a big sky for miles and the wind caressed her body like an old friend. She wondered what could be happening in the world outside of Roswell that night. She thought about the large cities she'd never seen before, and wondered if she ever would. Sometimes she thought about traveling, even if her small town life had its comforts. The largest city she'd seen was Phoenix a few times, but never anywhere as big as Los Angeles or New York. She remembered Christine mentioning her planned Honeymoon in Seattle at the World's Fair. *That* would've been something to see. Even though she truly knew it'd been Christine's choice to end her relationship with Jack, she partly felt responsible for holding her back on her dreams. It was a guilty feeling, but she only felt it for her sister. She couldn't care less what Jack had wanted. The man had never been kind to her. Wendy knew that is she further apologized for the stress her trauma may be causing; Christine would brush it off and tell her not to worry about it. She did this once, almost twice already. She hoped Christine wouldn't hold it against her somehow one day in the future. It was great they were getting along again, but remembered the years they were apart and when they argued. It was simply a woeful thought she didn't want to come to fruition.

Christine opened the back door of the house and the hinges creaked terribly, just as they'd always done for many years. Wendy stared ahead of herself at the sunset, which was nearly gone now. The rays of orange light where growing weaker in the clouds. Her sister handed her a small glass of ice tea, and Wendy took it in her hands by second nature.

"Doesn't it ever make you wonder...?" Wendy started to say, speaking softly in the night wind. Christine sat down on a vacant porch chair beside her, and leaned back to relax.

"Wonder what?" she asked her. Wendy's eyes gazed up into the large sky above them and were silently surveying the sheer vastness of the area. It was so quiet here...only the very faint sounds of distant cars in the town a few miles away. Sounds traveled further in spacious areas with little amounts of trees to absorb them.

"Wonder if...there are *other* worlds up there...*out there*...far away from here" Wendy whispered. Her voice was just audible enough for only the two of them to here. Christine looked up into the sky and sighed deeply in her chest. She thought for a moment, tilting her head as they watched a shooting star streak across the world. The stars were becoming more present now that the light was disappearing faster. Out in the desert, the light pollution was very dim, and sometimes not there at all. Wendy thankfully lived in a smaller neighborhood away from town where you could calmly stargaze without interference.

"I think there are worlds out there...yes. I don't know if we'll ever see them in our time, though. I remember granddad used tell me he thought about life on other planets when he was younger. Before he died, he used to tell me stories about mysterious objects in the sky. He would see them a lot as a kid, but no one ever believed him of course" Christine said. Her eyes dropped to the ground as Wendy listened intently. "...No one ever believes a child about things like that."

Wendy was surprised to hear this coming from Christine. Her sister was always the rational one, and looked for an explanation for anything unusual in life. She believed there was a solution to any problem, and thoughts of fantasy belonged to the minds of children. She knew Christine was talking about their grandfather. Their mother's father. He passed away in 1951 from pneumonia at the age of sixty. Their grandmother had died four years prior to his death from heart failure. She hadn't thought about him in years, but she remembered he was a thoughtful man who loved his meerschaum pipes. He would sit on this very porch and smoke well into the evening, humming old war tunes that used to play in the theater news reels during the 1940s. He was always closer to Christine for some reason. Wendy had always been the one to believe in fantasies and explorative stories, and yet…she didn't recall her grandfather ever telling these to her. Maybe it was because he knew she would surely believe them without a problem, and Christine was the one who needed convincing. Christine had tried to grow up sooner that she needed to. She never let herself be young when she was still young enough to do it. Many people did this during the war, and after it ended. Many were forced to grow up long before they needed to. Now, television news reels talked about nuclear prevention and the "space race". The world of tomorrow wasn't far behind them.

"I can still feel him…" Wendy spoke up, turning her head toward her sister. Christine narrowed her eyes and felt confused about what her sister was talking about.

"Feel who?" she questioned. Wendy let a small tear slip down her face and onto her clothing. The ice tea was making her hands feel cold and numb, but she didn't move them.

"Johnny…" she whispered again. "…he's inside my head…all the time now." She brought a hand up to her temple and held it there. She looked a bit dazed in dimming light, with her blue eyes glowing in the dark. "He won't go away."

Christine felt very nervous now. She swallowed hard and clenched her hands together, trying to find the words to reply to Wend who was sitting there somewhat eerily in the twilight. She knew her sister wasn't trying to scare her, but this talk of Johnny was becoming too frequent.

"Does…he say anything?" she asked her. She immediately regretted that decision, for it wasn't what she planned to say. Her curiosity was taking over.

"No" Wendy answered and shook her head. "I just see his face…and feel his presence. He's…trying to find me" she admitted. Christine leaned forward and took the glass from Wendy's hands. Setting on the small table between him, she looked directly into her sisters eyes with a serious vibe.

"I may know someone who can help" she said then, holding Wendy's hands together to warm them. "I...haven't seen him a while, but...I know he lives outside of town. He's an old friend" she told her. Wendy started to breathe heavily at the thought of this, wondering if her sister was going to send her away somewhere now.

"I'm not crazy Christine...I know what I saw the night I met him" she quickly countered. Her voice rose in panic, and Christine was already nodding her head.

"I know...and don't worry. He's not a doctor or anything. He's just a friend. I'm not sending you away, so get that thought out of your head right now" she replied with a directive tone. Wendy caught her breath for a moment, and then sighed in relief.

"O-Okay then" she said simply. She wiped her eyes and took a drink of her ice tea to calm herself. It spilled down her cheeks but she didn't seem to notice. Wendy felt like a mess. The thoughts of Johnny plagued her mind even more now. It truly felt like he was getting closer to finding her…*somehow*…remotely.

"We'll go see him tomorrow" Christine proposed. "I think he'll know what to do."

Chapter 11

It was the next day the two young women ventured out into the hot desert world again. Even though the policeman the day before had warned them to stay inside their home, the sisters had someone to meet. Someone who Christine apparently knew, and Wendy didn't know about. In fact, her sister was being quiet for almost the entire trip outside of town. She drove for close to twenty minutes south of Roswell on a dirt road that dirtied up the exterior of Christine's shiny little Nash. The red and white paint was quickly becoming the same color of light brown from the rocky dust. Wendy hoped they wouldn't get a flat tire driving over this road. She was sure the car had a spare, because she'd seen in the trunk before, but Wendy had never changed a tire in life. She was once stranded in town for almost an hour when her previous station wagon received a flat on her way home from work once. Thankfully, she was near civilization and it made the experience less stressful than it would've been, had she stopped in the middle of nowhere. Going out away from town like this made Wendy feel very uneasy. It flooded memories of Johnny and the Moonbeam Diner since she met them both in the middle of the desert that lonesome night. Christine kept the radio turned off to concentrate on the road.

"It's been a while since I've been out here, but...I'm sure they still live out here" she said then. Wendy turned her head as she glanced at her sister, all while steadying herself in the bumpy ride of the small vehicle.

"Who are "*they*"? she asked her, wanting better clarification. "You still haven't told me who we're meeting out here." Wendy was anxious and Christine knew this, yet for some reason she felt the need to keep their destination a secret.

"You'll see. Just relax, we're almost there now" she replied in confidence. "There's nothing to worry about right now."

Christine's reply was meant to calm her sister a bit more, but Wendy was feeling anything but calm. The countless cacti and scattered rock piles were the only scenery for miles around them. The road was thankfully visible, but it too was barely there to see. She could tell that few people used the road for traveling, but it was the only reassurance that they weren't in the center of a wilderness landscape. Was this road even named? She wasn't sure. There had never been a street name sign when they first got on this road. Maybe it was a private drive. Wendy began to count the little checkers on the design of her black and white dress that Christine had newly bought for her. It was done in a similar style to her old yellow and white polka-dot one she wore the night she met Johnny. Instead of going out to the clothing store with her sister a few days ago, Christine took the initiative to buy new clothes for her sister as a surprise. It turned out to be a nice gift, since Christine remembered what Wendy liked. Feeling somewhat dressed up, Wendy hoped the desert dust wouldn't get all over her new clothing. It was odd thought to be having in an anxious situation, but it was better than feeling worried about where they were going. Something to distract her mind as they drove along.

"There it is" Christine said finally, slowing the car as they approached a small turn in the dirt road ahead. A side road was leading off toward a small adobe house in the near distance. At the front of the turn, a tiny white mailbox read *Blackhawk Farm* across the side in bold lettering. Wendy stared at it as they rode passed the little box and headed toward the quaint home on the landscape. She was about to meet whoever Christine was talking about, and Wendy wasn't sure how to feel in this moment. All she could do was trust her sister now. Strangely, she didn't feel in danger, but sure feeling of apprehension and unpredictability was surrounded her body. The butterflies in her stomach weren't the comforting kind. Hopefully she wouldn't throw up from this twisted feeling, as it wouldn't make any first greeting a memorable one. Christine took Wendy's hand as the car came to a stop by the adobe house.

"It's alright, dear. You can relax. These are good people here" she said quietly with a smile. She turned off the engine of the car and the air was noticeably much quieter than before. The sound of the Nash driving along had vibrated Wendy's ears and the silence poked through them invasively. Wendy took a breath and watched the front door of the small home open gently as Christine stepped out of the car. She forced a tight smile as she got ready to meet the new person her sister told her about.

An older man stepped out of his home and stared ahead at the two women on his property.

He never made a sound as Christine approached him. In fact, he never left the front of the house, as though he felt guarded. It was clear to Wendy, that her sister knew this man, but what kind of connection they had was beyond her. She'd never met this man in her life, but before the trauma she experienced, Christine had known many people that she never told anyone else about. The older man had graying black hair that fell down to his shoulders, and a deep brown tone of skin that showed a series of wrinkles from his age of years of being in the sunlight. He wore a farmer's garb and black cowboy boots as he stood with his arms folded, puffing soft smoke rings that floated above his head. His dark brown eyes fixed heavily upon them. A pipe was in the corner of his mouth, perched perfectly in the edge. He clearly kept it there often.

"Hey there Chief" Christine greeted the man with a welcoming smile. "It's been a while since I seen ya last." She stood in front of him with her hands on her hips as Wendy hobbled up behind with her walking cane. Wendy quickly got the notion that this man was Native American, but she didn't know of what tribe he was from. Possibly none, since he seemed to live alone. The man nodded slowly to greet his company and a slight smile formed at the side of his mouth.

"Hello again, Miss. Yes…it has been some time since you have been here" he replied with a deep voice. The man seemed full of old wisdom and a very calm demeanor. He gave the vibe of being quite content with where he stood and how he lived. Not even new company would bother him.

"This is my sister, Wendy" Christine said, motioning to the young woman behind her while keeping eye contact with the man. "She's the one I told you about on the phone." The man gave another quiet nod to Wendy, and she did the same in return.

"Hello, sir" Wendy said delicately. Christine turned to her sister with the same smile.

"Wendy, this is Chief Blackhawk. He owns a cactus farm here" she explained. The man took his pipe out of his mouth and stepped toward them. The desert wind blew his hair away from his face and the girls could see him clearly now.

"You've come to see my son again, haven't you?" he asked directly. Christine nodded, and then took Wendy's hand.

"We both have. Is he still living here?" she questioned. The old farmer pointed toward the back of his home beyond the cactus beds. He then turned away again, and walked back into his home.

"You will find him out that way. He's should be done with his work now" the man informed before going back inside. Christine turned to her sister and gave her arm a tug to follow. Wendy moved sluggishly over the tiny rocks with her cane, so as not to fall.

"So...*he* was not the man we came to meet then?" she asked her. Still very curious as ever, with her blue eyes shining brightly in the sun. Christine walked forward, but slow enough for her sister to keep up with her.

"You'll see" was her only reply. Wendy felt somewhat annoyed at the secrecy. They were here now, so the least her sister could do was be informative. They continued on past the cactus beds of the farm where several species of cacti were growing at different height rates. Wendy recognized a few Saguaro cactuses and some prickly pears as well, and the tiny red and yellows flowers were beautiful on some of them. The old man clearly knew what he was doing, since they all looked healthy and strong. A cactus would grow slowly for many years, and some lived to be 150 years old. Wendy wondered how long the little farm had been out here. Probably since before she was born.

It was then…is the near distance…she could hear a sound drifting warmly across the wind like a dream. It was music. Very soothing…and relaxing music. Christine heard it too, and she motioned for her sister to stop moving. The two girls stood in there as they listened to the song floating closer to them. Wendy watched her sister stare ahead and she too, slowly turned her eyes upon a young man sitting quietly on the ground ahead of them. The sun passed behind a long cloud and the light dimmed enough for them to notice him there. He was a man, but much younger than his father they'd talked with before. His sat with his legs crossed, eyes closed and his exceptionally long and radiant black hair dangling down behind him to the ground. If Wendy had to guess…his hair would probably reach the back of his knees when he stood up. It draped down around his glossy bare chest of a lovely chestnut color and toned muscles after many years of working on the farm. He was playing a type of wood-wind instrument that she couldn't quite identify…but it was beautiful. *He*…was beautiful. The hawk feathers in hair blew gently in the wind while he played, and the sound was entrancing. He wore traditional native pants of a light brown leather, and felt content with no shoes to cover his feet.

He was one with nature.

The two young women gazed at him until he finished his song, lightly lowering his instrument to his lap and turning his deep brown eyes at them. They slowly gleamed in a warm hazelnut color when the light reflected on them.

"There he is…the handsome man, himself" Christine spoke, blushing at the sight of him. She caressed her long hair and brushed it aside as the man walked toward them. He stopped there, looking back and forth between the two and finally spoke with a genial voice that sounded heavenly to Wendy's ears.

"I'm Mohan" he said to her. He gave a tender smile and Wendy quickly felt relaxed. She couldn't believe how much she liked this man. She finally knew the "surprise" her sister was telling her about. For once…she'd met a man that Christine had also been attracted to. Usually all the men Christine knew absolutely disgusted Wendy in the past…but not this one. *He* was amazing to look at. His arms were very thick and strong. He could probably lift both Christine and

Wendy at the same time is what she thought to herself.

"Hi there, sexy…" Christine greeted with delight, "…it's been a long time since I seen you." Her voice was very flirtatious and Wendy was surprised at how forward she was acting toward this man. *Obviously*…she knew him from a time that she never told anyone about. Mohan Blackhawk cocked his head slightly, letting his hair fall to one side and his eyes glance away from her. He either felt shy or didn't take compliments well. Then again, Wendy's sister was often very forward with men she liked, so she might have made him feel uneasy. Still, he didn't leave and continued to speak with them. Maybe he expected this reaction from her.

"Yes it has" he replied calmly. He brought his hands together as he held his musical pipe in between them. "But I do remember you, Christine" he admitted. Christine gave a flirty laugh, and then turned toward her sister.

"This is Wendy, my younger sister. I brought her here to meet you" she presented. Wendy felt the need to scowl at Christine for mentioning the fact she was younger, and then realized it would've been an immature action. She suddenly felt like a young girl again, standing in front of this gorgeous young man. It was simply a sibling rivalry. She almost felt jealous that Christine knew him and never said anything...and yet, they clearly weren't together in a relationship. Maybe something prevented that from blossoming in the past.

Mohan looked upon Wendy with keen interested and he cocked his head curiously some more with blinking eyes. He clearly loved to do this. He reminded Wendy of a cat in this way, and it almost made her giggle. She then noticed how serious the man was becoming and he gently took her hands into his own after placing his instrument into a little pouch pocket strapped to his pants. He gazed deeply into Wendy's blue eyes as though to tell her something very important.

"You have seen them...haven't you?" he quietly questioned, holding her hands close to his body. The motion brought her body close to his own and she felt immersed in his presence. He was so dominant...but not in an overbearing way. He was like a leader that demanded respect...but as gentle as a rabbit. She would follow his every motion.

"Who do you mean?" Wendy asked him then. Mohan titled his head forward as his eyes loomed at her. His whisper was delicate, but had a serious feel to it.

"The shadow men...you have seen them..." he replied, "...I *know* you have."

His hands were hot from the blazing sun, but they warmed Wendy's skin nicely in his touch. There was something special about this young man. Something very different than the average human being. He had a power among himself. A natural gift within his mind. He knew things that other's did not...and he knew them before people could say them.

"Wendy...," Christine started to say, as the man gazed upon her sister, "...Mohan is a psychic. I brought you here...because he *knows*. He knows what you have been through...and he can understand you better than I can" she informed. Wendy's eyes widened at the sound of this information. Mohan's comforting gazed was calming to see, and he held a sense of sincerity about him that couldn't be ignored.

"One of them is seeking you...isn't he?" Mohan asked again. Wendy swallowed, and nodded to him without speaking. "And...there is another...*another one*...that follows. He follows you, but...his intentions are noble" Mohan explained. Christine looked at Mohan curiously. She wondered if the "another one" he spoke of was the man known as Mr. White.

"Yes" was all Wendy could say, but it was all Mohan needed to continue. He focused on Wendy's aura and touched her spirit with his own. The air felt warm and safe. This was the safest feeling she'd experienced in a very long time. In fact...she'd never felt this safe in a man's presence...*ever*... in her entire life up to this point.

"He is noble...but he cannot show it very well. He's still learning the ways of people" Mohan clarified. Wendy knew he was speaking of Mr. White. The mysterious man in the black suit still frightened her at the thought of him, but what Mohan was saying about him was very intriguing indeed. Maybe there was something about Mr. White that she didn't understand yet, and would later come to discover in time. Even so...the man was stalking her, and she didn't feel comfortable with it.

"And...w-what about...J-Johnny?" Wendy asked him, slightly stuttering her words. Mohan's eyes narrowed darkly at the mention of this other name. He wasn't angry with Wendy, but she could tell he knew what kind of "being" Johnny truly was.

"He…is selfish one…and *very* dangerous. He only seeks to please himself. To please his…*hunger"* Mohan said. His voice darkened just as his gaze, but he carefully led Wendy along with him as he began to walk. "Come…sit with me" he told her. "We must prepare."

The young man lead Wendy over to the spot where he'd been sitting before, and a small fire was burning on the ground below them. The two girls hadn't noticed it there before. Mohan had been relaxing it by it when they arrived. Christine followed in her own curiosity and spoke up quickly.

"Prepare for what, Mohan?" she questioned, sitting down on the ground with them. The three of them sat in a triangular shape, with Wendy feeling a bit odd knowing her prosthetic leg couldn't bend right. She instead, let it face outward while Mohan and Christine sat with their legs together.

"Prepare to see him again. Wendy will face him very soon…and she will see the follower again too." Mohan declared. He was very sure of his words, and very delicate about saying them. Even though the thought of facing Johnny again weighed heavily on her mind, Wendy felt comforted by

Mohan's presence...and was eager to hear what he had to say.

     The ground where the three of them sat together was smoothed nicely in a small circle. In the center of the circle was the little fire burning steadily. Wendy's curious mind figured this spot was used often by Mohan to relax and possibly pray to his deities. There was a series of short poles in the ground with decorative masks placed over them, turned to face the fire. They weren't directly beside them, but aligned the circle they currently sat in. Wendy asked no questions about them. Each one was very intricate and beautiful. They seemed to be hand-made and possibly by Mohan, himself. Whether they served as decoration or for chanting, she didn't know. She felt herself smiling being surrounded by this man's culture. He was fascinating in every way, and so collected with himself. His father had been calm, but Mohan was clearly in positive spirits. His mood was peaceful and posed no threat to anything around him. The clouds were gathering over them in the sky, but they didn't seem to be passing rain. It was nice to have the sun blocked even temporarily.

Mohan laid his arms outward over his knees as he sat contently beside the two women. He closed his eyes and breathed gently in and out to keep himself relaxed. His chest looked rather nice when his did this, Wendy thought. They way it moved in and out kept her eyes fixed upon him. Even though she could probably gaze at him for hours, she forced herself to remember why she and Christine came here to begin with. They were here to receive help and insight to her situation. It was Christine who spoke up first, but not impatiently. She seemed to know just when to do it. Mohan never showed any sign of annoyance. He was ready for anything.

"What does Johnny want from my sister?" Christine asked him, holding her hands together in front of her lap in a polite manner. She was staring right at Mohan without blinking until he finally answered her. The young man held his eyes closed and kept his body completely still. He seemed to be meditating, but Wendy figured he was connecting to their minds with his own to see into the future. Isn't that what *all* psychics do? Wendy wasn't sure, but she let him do whatever he needed in order to help her.

"His name is not Johnny…" Mohan began to say, keeping his eyes shut lightly, "…and he is not of this world."

Wendy slowly brought her hands together as she listened, letting her sister ask the questions until she felt it was the right time for her to speak. Christine seemed to have more experience with this than she did. Maybe Mohan had done this with Christine before in the past. Probably the last time they met.

"What *is* Johnny…and where is he from?" Christine asked again, leaning in closer than before. She entangled her fingers together like an excited child, but she it wasn't excitement she was feeling…it was dread. Mohan twitched his eyes for a moment and tilted his head. His breathing was becoming quicker now.

"He is…from another world. One that is close to ours, but…we cannot see it. A world *beside* our own…where creatures of his kind live and die…just like *our*s do" he explained. His voice, now a bit shaken, but continuously focused while he felt his mind reaching outward around them. Both girls were becoming worried now as Mohan revealed more about who Johnny was and where he came from. Mohan's information was vague, yet strangely alluring. They somehow knew he was telling the truth without seeing it completely. "He has been in our world for a long time…" he continued, turning his head the opposite direction now, taking in a deep breath and letting it out before he finished, "…he lures in others with his kindness…and has taken many forms. He is very convincing."

Wendy leaned toward Mohan and finally spoke softly to him, and watched his head turn to face her as she did this. He seemed to know exactly when she'd speak to him right then.

"Why does he want…*me?*" she questioned, feeling a bit scared now after hearing what he'd been saying. Mohan took another deep breath to steady himself and he slowly opened his brown eyes to look at her.

"Because…you got away. You left him there…*hungry*….and waiting" he informed, clutching the tops of his knees. Mohan almost seemed to be in pain, but if he was, he didn't clarify it. Christine noticed this as well, and she reached over to calm him down again by placing her hands over his body. She began to rub his chest and back carefully, and not in a sexual manner. She only sought to comfort him.

"What should do? Will he ever leave me alone?" Wendy asked once more. Mohan, clearly shaking from so much concentration, answered with a tired voice and a whisper. His response made Wendy feel terrible for putting him through this experience just to help her, even if he was willing to do. He was exhausting himself.

"D-Don't...l-let him s-see your f-fear...th-that is what he w-wants" he said finally, leaning into Christine's arms as he caught his breath again. Wendy reached over to him with tears in her eyes and gently rubbed his arm as she whispered to him.

"Thank you, Mohan...thank you for everything" she told him, feeling guilty of having put him through this, and deciding not to ask anything further of him. The young man simply nodded and formed a tired smile. His breathing was nearly back to normal now, and he was regaining his strength.

"I must rest now" he told them, starting to stand again. He helped Wendy up from the ground and Christine followed. "Please be careful going home...there are eyes watching all around you" he informed them.

"Will you be alright?" Wendy asked as they began to walk back toward the farm. The sun was peeking through the clouds with tiny rays of light shining down on them. They felt warmer than the air was, and the clouds were beginning to move on.

"I am fine, Miss Wendy" he told her calmly. His eyes, though tired from loss of energy, were happy and warm. "I feel glad to have met you" he told her directly. Wendy blushed a bit, but continued to walk with him back to his home where his father was waiting. The old man still had his pipe in his mouth, and he took it out to address them.

"Mohan...you must not tire yourself like this..." he said to his son. Mohan's eye looked at his father with a short blink and where wide for a brief moment.

"I'm alright, father. These women needed my help...as you know" he clarified. Chief Blackhawk gave a sigh, which seemed stern by the sound of it, but then he relaxed his face. He was merely concerned for his son's safety. He knew that his "gift" drained his energy whenever he used it to help others gain foresight about their future, or their past experiences. Today, Mohan had looked into both for Wendy...and the result was rather strenuous for him.

"Go inside and rest, my son. Tomorrow is another day's work" he told him. Mohan nodded to his father, and turned to Wendy and Christine once more before going inside the house. Even though he was indeed a man, he held respect to his elder and listened to him well.

"Take great care...and come to me again if you need to. I will be waiting" he said to them with a tender smile. Wendy watched him leave with his father following behind. Christine gave a wave to the both of them and started walking toward the car again with Wendy beside her.

"Don't worry, Wendy...he will be just fine. He's a strong man" Christine told her confidently. Wendy wasn't sure what to say. She sat herself in the vehicle and stared at the dashboard until the hum of the engine vibrated all around her.

"Do you and Mohan ever...*you know*...date?" she questioned, not knowing what to say. Christine backed the car up and turned it around again as she followed the same dirt road back toward Roswell. She drove carefully on the way out and waited a few minutes before answering.

"No...we never did. I wanted to but,...he didn't want the same" she answered. Christine's reply wasn't out of sadness, no resentment. She genuinely seemed pleased with seeing Mohan again and helping Wendy gain some insight about her problem.

"How come?" Wendy asked again. "He seemed very comfortable around you."

Christine laughed a bit, but not because she thought anything was funny. She sighed and gave Wendy an answer she wasn't expecting.

"I don't think he likes women...in *that* way. But...I could be wrong. Maybe he's just very reserved and polite. He actually seemed very interested in *you*, Wendy" Christine explained. Wendy was surprised to hear both of these things. Was Mohan...a homosexual? Or...was he just very content with himself, and not seeking anyone? Surely he wasn't interested in Wendy, she thought to herself. It felt weird to think about herself in somewhat third person, but she couldn't see how an attractive man such as Mohan would be interested in a young woman who just came out of a coma some months ago and was now missing a leg. She hadn't even felt she was attractive enough anymore for *any* man to want her. She genuinely felt very undesirable.

"I don't think he wants me…like that" Wendy confessed. "I'm not very desirable." Christine looked at her sister suddenly and seen her staring out the window with a sullen expression. She realized just how much Wendy despised her own appearance, and had very little self-confidence. This was most likely due to the fact she'd survived such a terrible ordeal, and had one of her legs surgically removed. She probably felt like an outcast now. Christine had been very sympathetic toward her sister ever since deciding to help take care of her after what happened, but she knew that she could never truly understand how Wendy felt inside her head without having the same experience as her. She took her sister's hand and held it gently as the sight of Roswell appeared in the distance. They were almost back in town now, and Christine felt the need to drop the subject. It's odd how the trip back home always seems shorter than the trip to your destination. When in reality, it's usually the same length of time going back.

"I love you, Wendy. I will always be here for you…don't worry" she reassured her. Wendy made a sigh, and turned to her sister with a weak smile. She believed Christine of course, but her pressing thoughts still weighed upon her like a rock.

"I love you too, sis" she replied. "Let's go home and eat something good."

Christine nodded to her sister at the thought of food. Their breakfast had been small that day, and the both of them were getting hungry by now. They couldn't go to Blackhawk Farm until the afternoon, since the men who lived there needed to do morning chores, so they were both in need of a lunch now.

"Sounds good to me" she agreed. The car drove onto the main road now, and the sign of civilization was all around them. Wendy hoped…after what Mohan had told them…they weren't truly being watched this very moment. It was a crawling feeling she didn't want, but couldn't help wonder about it.

Chapter 12

Wendy had never been someone who had a general opinion on psychic people, or people who claimed to have any other type of paranormal ability or encounters. She wasn't closed minded to the idea, she just simply had not witnessed anyone who was psychic until recently. Honestly, she was now even more open minded to believing in *many* forms of the unknown or unexplained after what she'd went through. The world was now an unusual dream unfolding different scenarios every day. Common ghost stories now seemed very simple. It was also surprising just how easily Christine had believed in Mohan as well, considering she'd always been a more rational-thinking person. Perhaps it was because she was attracted to him, she could believe him easier...and because he was right about Wendy's situation. She wondered what it must be like to have an ability like that. When to use it...and when *not* to use it?

She was sure that many people would abuse that power, but Mohan didn't seem to be one of those people. He was a tranquil young man, and very sincere. His peaceful face was one she'd never forget for a long time, even if they never met again in the future.

Stopping at a red-light, the women noticed traffic building up on the main avenues of Roswell now that they were back in town. It was just that time of day again. An even bigger swarm of cars would jam the streets in the early evening later that day as people drove home from work. Many folks think small towns don't have traffic build-up, but Roswell had surprisingly increased in popularity in the recent years with more frequent visitors. The town itself had grown a bit more since the last time Wendy had seen it. She previously noticed many newer stores and shops after coming home again from the months in the hospital.

A line of cars drove up behind Christine's little Nash as they waited for the traffic light to change. She looked in her side mirror out of curiosity and noticed one of them to be fairly long and black in color. The light shone brightly off its windshield about three cars back behind them. She couldn't tell who was driving the dark vehicle, but she slowly began to recognize it as the same black Edsel that Mr. White drove the day before. He was following them. Christine impatiently looked up the stoplight which *still* had not changed. Wendy touched her sister's arm to get her attention.

"What's wrong, sis?" she asked her quietly. Without looking away from the rear-view mirror, Christine spoke up in a soft but worried whisper.

"It's him, Wendy…Mr. White. He's following us just a few cars back" she informed. Wendy's eyes widened and she turned to head to look out the back window of the car without hesitation. Staring through her new cat's eye glasses, she watched as Mr. White's daunting black car slowly came into full view after the stoplight finally changed. The other cars behind them either turned off or moved into side lanes of the road. He sped up the car as he followed them and his pale face emerged hauntingly behind the windshield when the sunlight shifted. His emotionless gaze stared directly at them with determination. The girls weren't anywhere near the police station either, and Mr. White seemed to know this. He was following much closer than before…and he'd probably been doing so since they'd entered town again.

"Wendy…" Christine started to say, as she pressed the gas pedal a little harder to speed up, "…don't stare at him" she directed her. Wendy *did* watch him for another minute, but then turned back to face the front again.

"What'll we do!?" she asked in a worried tone. Her eyes were large and glassy, and her breath had increased. Christine softly shushed her sister to calm her as they drove on through the town. She turned onto a side street, and tried to make her way toward the police station again away from traffic.

"Shh…just stay calm. He won't get us" she assured her. Wendy wasn't convinced as she looked back out the rear window again, ignoring her sister's request. Strangely, Mr. White's car was a bit further behind, but still following them. It must've been Christine's sudden turn that distracted him before. With less traffic around them, they could possibly get away faster…but that also meant he could catch up to them easier.

"Just try and get to the police again" Wendy told her, attempting to catch her breath. Christine's kept her focus on the road and often glanced through the mirror at the same time. The following specter of a man was very much distracting her, and she nearly hit a parked car.

Swerving quickly away from it, the both of them heard a loud bang, like the sound of a gunshot, followed by a fierce jolt of the car sagging slightly to one side in the front. It was on Wendy's front passenger side, and Christine fought to steady the car as she brought it to a halt in the center of the street. Quickly jumping out the driver's side, Christine observed a flat tire just below where Wendy sat.

"God damn it!" she exclaimed, running her hands up through her hair stressfully. She opened Wendy's door as she saw Mr. White's Edsel looming nearer and yanked her sister out of the car.

"We gotta go! Now!" she yelled at her. They left the little car's engine running and the doors open as they hurriedly ran toward a building near their left side. The sound of muffled music was inside, and there seemed to be a crowd of people having some sort of party on the opposite side of the metal door facing them. Wendy rushed in a state of panic as her sister pulled her along. Her leg twisted a few times on the pavement, but she kept up with her as best she could. The crutch buckled and she began to carry it rather than walk with it.

"Slow down!" she demanded. "I can't go as fast as you!" Christine grabbed her sister's body completely, nearly lifting her off the ground as she brought her up on the sidewalk. She then ran over to the door of the building and opened it. The sound of music flooded into the street and into their ears. Both Wendy and Christine stepped into a large group of teenagers and young adults dancing around to LaVern Baker's song *"Voodoo, Voodoo"* in the center of the room. The room itself appeared to be an old gymnasium of sorts, or simply a large room for private parties. A full blown sock-hop party was underway, and the rock n' roll music filled the air in a deafening state. Wendy could just barely hear Christine demanding her to follow her as they made their way through the crowd. From behind them, Mr. White was already in the same room and following as best he could without being knocked over by rambunctious teens. Several rows of poodle skirts twirled around the room from young girls being lead by their boyfriends in the dance. The song was a very upbeat number, and distracting enough for most people not to notice the newcomers who'd entered the room. Wendy nearly screamed when she noticed Mr. White following them, and she began to push people out of her way along with her sister.

"We gotta get out of here! He's right behind us!" she exclaimed loudly. Mr. White's face was straight and expressionless. He was clearly confident that he had them cornered in this room now. Christine glanced around the people until she found another doorway at the opposite end of the room. It wasn't far from them, but the ocean of teenagers made it seem like a mile away. It was surely an exit out of this madness.

"C'mon!" she shouted out. "I see a way out from here!" Dragging Wendy along with her again as they pushed through the crowd. Many of the teens glared at them with looks of sudden anger as the two women made their way through. Several of them calling out *"Hey!"* and *"Watch it!"* as they came closer to the exit. Mr. White was very close now. Wendy could see him in her side vision when she turned her head slightly. She tried to keep up with Christine, but they were moving too fast. She fell sideways against a young man dancing nearby, and he thankfully caught her in his arms.

"Hey there, baby!" he called out to her. His smile was wide and his eyes were glassed from being drunk. Clearly, this party was unsupervised. The young man's breath was atrocious and his hair was greased up in the style of Elvis Presley. He now seemed very interested in Wendy's body lying against him. Christine forcefully pushed the boy aside and took her sister by the arm. Wendy was beginning to feel like a ragdoll being dragged around, and it was *very* uncomfortable.

"She ain't interested in you, now back off!" Christine demanded. The boy did indeed back up, but kept his wild grin as he took a big swig of his beer from the bottle he'd been holding. Wendy noticed Mr. White coming closer and she reacted without a second thought to defend herself when he reached forward. She quickly swung her crutch at him with all her might and it struck the side of his head with a loud thud. The man in the black suit came crashing down to the floor and several people soon screamed and gasped loudly in the room. The sudden danger sent the party into a crazed panic when the music stopped, and Mr. White stood up again. Wendy's mouth slowly dropped and her eyes widened as she stared directly at the man's grimace. His eyes…*weren't human.* The black sunglasses he'd worn before were now broken on the floor, and his secret was revealed. Many of the girls in the room saw them too and were screaming to get away from him. They were horrified at the sight of his solid black ovals reflecting the light of room as his silvery pupils pierced through their centers. The normally white areas of his eyes were very dark, and shown no sign of commonality that he was a being from this world. His eyes were now panicking and his red irises darted back and forth at everyone rushing away from him. The glow of his silver pupils made them appear much brighter in the light. His once emotionless face was now worried and he tried to cover himself in shame. He grabbed his hat from the floor, and reached into his pocket for a spare pair of sunglasses. Wendy had successfully distracted the man long enough for them to escape out the other door of the room. Leaving Mr. White behind as he frantically looked around for them. He then ran toward the door and flung it open…only to discover the two women had fled the scene and where nowhere to be found. Calmly, he placed the new shades over his inhuman ovals and began to walk away down the street as if nothing had happened. He knew the police would soon arrive on the scene, and that would be needless attention. It appeared that Wendy's attack had only stunned him, and he was quickly able to recover from it.

Making their way across the street and into a nearby park, Christine ran up to a nearby phone booth standing among some trees near a park bench. They had successfully escaped Mr. White by fleeing down the road, even though they'd left the car behind. Christine's first reaction was to call the police as Wendy sat down on the bench to rest. Reaching for the telephone receiver, she jumped at the sudden sound of its loud ring when an incoming call came unexpectedly. It made her stand there in surprise until she slowly picked it up. Answering with a soft *hello* she waited for a response. At first, it was merely static...but the sound of Mr. White's voice spoke through it...asking for Wendy. Christine then handed the phone to her sister whom was standing behind her now, reaching for it. Wendy wanted to hear what he had to say, even if Christine tried to shield him from her.

"Miss Fields...I am not here to harm you" Mr. White said calmly over the phone. He voice very clear now, and reminded her of a radio announcer about to read the news. She now knew that his strange voice was a result of him trying to mimic those of people he'd once heard before. To *blend in* with everyone else.

"What are you?!..." Wendy questioned in a harsh tone. Her voice was shaken and she could barely catch her breath. "Why are you following me?!"

Several police cars soon surrounded the area of the dance party as their sirens filled their air. They were a block away from the scene near the edge of the park, and she could see them in the distance from where she stood at the phone booth. The heat of the sun was making her sweat profusely and she wiped her forehead, drenching her hand in it.

"He is not going to stop desiring you, Miss Fields. He wants you more than anything now that you've got away from him" Mr. White explained carefully. She knew he was talking about Johnny now. The creature who disguised himself at the diner was still alive and desiring her. Her fears of him entering her mind in her dreams and thoughts were true. Mohan had clarified this as well. It was all becoming too stressful and her tears began to stream down her cheeks.

"What am I supposed to do?! I...don't even know if you're human!" she yelled at him over the phone. A silence followed her voice, but Mr. White spoke up again from wherever he was in that moment. Somewhere near the area so as not to be noticed by police. Christine clutched her sister's shoulders and tried to comfort her, and then reached for the phone. Wendy stopped her without speaking, preferring to hear the man's answer.

"I have to vanquish him, Miss Fields. That is evident now…and is also why I am here" Mr. White explained. His reply was simple and to the point. He was sure of himself and his duty. "I am not the only one who seeks him. This creature has revolted…and must be stopped. His murderous hunger does not belong in this world."

Mr. White's message made Wendy's eyes open more clearly as she listened. Her breath was coming easier now and she stood there quietly. If this man was trying to *kill* Johnny…then maybe he was an ally after all. It would certainly explain why Mohan said his intentions were "noble" during his psychic reading. Staring down at the floor of the phone booth, she cleared her throat and questioned him again.

"Why should I trust you when you've been stalking me? How do I know you're not going to harm me or my sister?" she asked him plainly. Her response was weak in sound, but direct enough to show her seriousness.

"My job is not to harm you, Miss Fields…and I take my job seriously. *Very* seriously." Mr. White explained. The last part of his reply was much slower than the rest of it, indicating he had no desire to change his plans. "I am following you, because you are the only person in over thirty years...to escape this creature's grasp. He does not let his prey leave willingly. He is *very* adamant about that. I have been watching him for quite some time...he evades me often...and he must be stopped. *With*...or *without*...your help."

Wendy raised her head up again, noticing the police ushering people out of the building as they evacuated the party. Christine watched the scene as she listened to Mr. White's voice from over the phone, as she could hear it faintly from where she stood.

"Are you an alien?" Wendy asked directly, staring at the scene of teenagers being arrested for drinking illegally.

"No, Miss Fields...I am not what you would call...an *alien"* he admitted. His reply was genuine, and he didn't seem to be lying about it.

"Then what are you? I know you're not human, Mr. White" Wendy said seriously. She was much calmer than before, still sweating droplets down the side of her face and smearing her make-up. A gentle wind blew through the area giving much needed relief.

"I am the same as him…the only difference is…I don't eat *people"* Mr. White confessed. His reply wasn't sarcastic, nor was he eager to explain himself. He generally just answered Wendy's question…and it gave her thoughts many possibilities to rethink everything up to this point. *Everything*…about her life…and the world around her. She dropped the phone receiver and slowly backed away from the booth in shock. Christine noticed her sister's reaction and tried to get a response from her.

"What?! What's wrong?!" she asked quickly. Wendy held her breath for nearly a minute and finally let it out again. She turned to her sister and answered with a whisper.

"He and Johnny…are the *same thing.* They're the same kind of…*monster…*but he doesn't want to hurt us" she explained. Christine caught her own breath, but suddenly became very demanding.

"Then what is he doing here?!" she asked roughly. Grabbing her sister's arms as Wendy stood there without being phased by it. Christine then took the phone in her hand, and listened to the droning sound of an empty line on the other end. Mr. White had hung up.

"He wants to kill Johnny…" Wendy said, looking over at the policemen again. "…and he wants my help to find him."

PART THREE

JOHNNY ANGEL

Chapter 13

The evening sky was blackened that night with an unexpected event. No twilight for the sun to set on the famous orange horizon in the west. No stars to glow from the vast ocean of space. A howling dust storm blew into Roswell, causing several districts to lose power and hold citizens inside their homes. Their only choice was to wait it out, and cancel all their evening plans. Most hadn't even eaten dinner yet, and could only make meals if their stove was gas powered. Even so, the dust crept through the window sills and under the doors, making everything unsanitary. It was a powerful one this time. They could only hope it would be gone by morning. These infamous tempests usually didn't last long, but on some occasions they could blow around for a week or more. The local news forecast reported tornado activity in the nearby state of Texas, which was common for them, and New Mexico was feeling the aftermath of its windy neighbor. The rocky dust of the New Mexican desert thankfully wasn't rushing into Wendy and Christine's home very much, since they had plenty of time to shut the windows and doors, and they placed some towels near the bottom of the main entrance of the home to help keep the particles out. When living in Roswell, the townsfolk had expected this to happen once in a while, and attempt to adapt to their living situations just like anyone else in their areas. In the northern states, people dealt with the snow every winter. In the west, people dealt with the earthquakes. It was the same for the people of the southeast, and their frequent hurricane season. No area of the Earth is without its random or reoccurring weather patterns. As humans, we've had to live *alongside* nature...rather than dominating it, just like we had dominated the planet itself. It's the one thing our species could not conquer while living here...and probably never will.

Wendy and Christine sat in the living room with a series of candles placed along the mantle of the fireplace, and on the coffee table. This lit up the room brightly enough to see each other's faces as they played card games in the dark. Sometimes it was hard to see the colors of the cards, and their games were played slowly. It was their only entertainment aside from reading books by candlelight or telling ghost stories. *That* was something they didn't need right now...but humans are always fascinated by the unknown. It was almost inevitable they would bring up some kind of ghostly conversation at some point. When surrounded by darkness in the night, the mind starts to wander outside of its natural self. It begins to explore...and become overwhelmed with paranoia. This can be easily avoided for most people, but for those with wilder imaginations, it can be haunting and unpredictable. For Wendy and Christine, it didn't matter if their minds were on full alert or not. They'd been experiencing things that most people never would understand, and this made them both feel very isolated together. Now, they were trapped within their home...with almost no means of escape. If anything were to happen...they'd be all on their own.

Laying down what she figured was the ace of diamonds on the small card pile in front of her, Christine softly spoke in the silence of the room. Outside, the vicious winds rattled the glass of the home's windows, and branches from the yucca trees could be heard as they scrapped against the outer walls and the roof.

"We might have to clean the car tomorrow after the storm" she said gently, looking over the cards in hand. She was rearranging them according to suits, and squinting her eyes to see the colors. Wendy laid down a card of her own and replied without looking up.

"It's not your car though...you can just take it back to the rental place and they'll clean it" she said simply. Christine shrugged her shoulders and nodded slightly as she placed another card.

"Yeah, I suppose" she replied quietly. A sudden bang struck the roof of the house right then, but the girls merely flinched lightly. Most likely the sound of a flying branch. It wasn't as bad as the ones from earlier that made them literally jump at every sound. The storm had been in progress for hours now ever since they'd got back home. Earlier in the day, Christine had her little Nash towed away to a car shop to have its tire changed. The dust storm had been reported when they arrived at the shop, and the mechanic told them to come back the next morning to retrieve the vehicle just to be safe. Until then, Christine had rented a car for the night. A nice '57 Mercury Turnpike Cruiser of daffodil yellow in color. It was still in good condition for a car of six years old now. Wendy had admired the car's styling on the ride home. She liked its unique taillight design, and only hoped she could one day drive a car again. She missed her station wagon, and her insurance said they'd help with another vehicle once she was medically ready to drive again. Unfortunately, this wouldn't be for a while, maybe over another year or so until she was used to walking with her new leg completely again. It was getting easier every day, but it still had its difficulties. She would have to find a new doctor again as well, ever since the recent death of Dr. Eli Patterson. It was also a real possibility that Wendy may never drive a vehicle ever again, and Christine would have to drive her to places. As much as she didn't want this reality, she was slowly beginning to accept it.

"It's a shame you gotta take it back tomorrow. It's a pretty car. I really like it" Wendy spoke again, continuing the conversation. When in a situation such as this, with very little to do, casual conversations could be about anything. This was surely the longest the two sisters had ever talked about a car. Especially one they didn't even own.

"I know. You've always liked big cars" Christine added. "Maybe once you're able to walk on your own again, we can get you a new one" she proposed. Wendy made a soft sigh, and laid down another card on the table. This was probably the eight game of rummy they played tonight.

"That's not going to happen, Christine. We both know that" Wendy declared. "I can't even run to save myself." Her voice held a certain depressive tone to it that made Christine want to drop the subject. She knew Wendy wasn't the type to go on feeling sorry for herself, but she didn't want to argue either. If Wendy felt this way about it, then she understood why. She would've probably felt the same way too.

Christine continued to sit there on the floor, staring down the cards on the coffee table without speaking. Wendy lifted her eyes, and after yet another sigh she set her hands down on her lap.

"I'm sorry…it's just…everything is very…difficult lately" she told her quietly. Christine set her cards down and looked across at her sister, nodding to her in acceptance.

"No, it's fine. I'm not angry really…I just wish you had more confidence in yourself. But I know you're not feeling it much after everything that's happened" Christine admitted. Wendy took off her cat's eye glasses and rubbed her forehead between her eyes to soothe a tension pain.

"Yeah I know" she continued, "and after what Mr. White told me today…I'm not sure of a lot of things now" she said. Christine gathered the cards together on the table, indicating she was done with the game. Another gust of wind blew around the house with an eerie chilling sound. Wendy looked at the up and noticed the living room ceiling fan shaking lightly with the rumbles of the home.

"I hope the vibrations don't knock the roof down on us when we sleep" she announced. Wendy took a sip of ice water that'd been sitting nearby all this time, and sweating from condensation.

"I doubt it. This house has been around for decades. One of the oldest in our neighborhood" she proclaimed, indicating it had weathered many storms before this one. Wendy took a drink of her own water glass and watched the tiny flames on the candles dance in the breeze they made between themselves. Christine folded her arms as the two of them sat there.

"Do you believe him?" she asked, gaining Wendy's attention.

"Believe who?" Wendy replied with her own question.

"You know…Mr. White. Do you believe him?" Christine questioned, referring the phone call earlier that day. Wendy hadn't thought about whether or not she believed him. He just seemed like a believable person…or alien. Whatever he truly was.

"I guess so" she told her, beginning to stack the playing cards into a small structure out of boredom. "What choice do I have, but to believe him?"

Christine unfolded her arms and felt dissatisfied with her sister's answer. She wasn't sure what she was looking for from her by asking this, but they didn't quite feel like they were on the same page, so to say. Wendy was acting unusually calm about the situation. She either had accepted the fact they spoke with an otherworldly being, or the reality just hadn't sunk in completely. Maybe it was her way of trying to move on and forget about it. It seemed odd to her for someone who experienced a trauma to simply act so calm, but maybe she was tired of remembering it. Christine took one of the cards and began to help her sister build the little house in progress.

"What about Johnny? Do you believe he's still trying to find you?" she asked her. It was then, Wendy stopped moving and Christine noticed this. Her sister was staring at her blankly as if to scorn her for daring to bring up the topic of Johnny again. To Christine's surprise, Wendy simply swallowed and looked back down.

"I don't know" she whispered. Her response was barely audible at all in the silent room, other than the sound of the storm. Christine had mostly read her sister's lips to know what she said. It was enough. Christine hated seeing her sister act this way, and she knew deep in her mind that something had to be done. Even if she had to go and find Johnny, herself, she would help her sister to feel happy once again. It wasn't right for Mr. White to pester Wendy for help in his *duty* of stopping this Johnny character. He should either do it himself, or ask for Christine's assistance. Wendy was in no condition to do anything but recover quietly in her own home. She was neither physically stable nor in the right mind set to approach this problem, and the thought of Johnny getting close to her again would only make everything worse. *If...*Johnny truly existed or not. It was another thought that had been plaguing Christine's mind ever since she heard Wendy speak his name. Did Johnny truly exist...or was it all a made-up sequence that her mind fabricated from being damaged in a terrible car accident? She didn't want to think her sister was lying, and in fact, she didn't think so. She *was*, however, willing to believe the existence of Johnny was created by Wendy's unconscious mind. Even if both Mohan and Mr. White had mentioned him. In fact, it was only because of Mohan that Christine considered believing in Johnny's existence. It was such a contradictive feeling. Mr. White wasn't enough to convince her. His actions were very secretive and unpredictable up until recently when he divulged information to Wendy over the phone…and *only*….to Wendy. Christine was beginning to realize that she felt she would need to *see* Johnny in order to believe in his existence completely.

Wendy had stopped moving. She was no longer stacking cards as she looked at her sister curiously, as if trying to decipher what she'd been thinking.

"What?" Christine then asked, looking up at her. Wendy's face slowly frowned and her eyes held a sense or worry to them.

"You…don't believe me…do you?" she asked. They way she said it didn't make it sound like a question, but more like a sullen statement.

She already knew the answer. Christine sighed, continuing to build the house of cards even after Wendy stopped.

"I do but...I don't think Mr. White should be bothering you to help him. You've been through enough already" she said directly. Wendy leaned back, turning away from the situation, trying to find the strength to stand up on her own. She'd already been sitting on the floor for an hour or more, and her body was tired of the constant still position. Even though she agreed with what Christine had just said, she knew her sister didn't truly believe her.

"I should've known this would happen..." she started to say, attempting to prop herself up to standing with her crutch, "...you're all I have left, Christine. They least you can do is believe me after everything I've told you. Even after Mohan and Mr. White and have told you" Wendy said with slight tone of anger. She wasn't yelling or raising her voice, but her manner was enough to tell Christine that she was upset now. Her sister didn't raise her voice either, but continued to approach the situation.

"Have you met Mr. White before?" she asked, not bothering to stand up. Wendy stopped moving at looked at her sister as though she'd grown three heads on her shoulders.

"What the hell kind of question is that?" she asked her, feeling appalled.   Christine shrugged her shoulders and stacked another card on her tiny house.

"Just wondering. It's hard to trust a lot of things now, and I'm only trying to make sense of our situation, Wendy" she admitted. Wendy finally stood up completely, without the aid of her sister and leaned against her crutch.

*"No, Christine...*I haven't met him before. And if I had, why would I hit him with a crutch to protect us in front of a hundred teenagers?" she said, raising her voice higher now. It wasn't just because of the storm either. Wendy made sure to let her sister know just how stupid her question seemed to her. Christine stared at her sister for a moment, and then nodded gently in agreement. She dropped the cards and stood up to be on the same eye level with her.

"You're right...and I'm sorry. I'm only trying to make sense of things...that's all. I *do* believe you, but...I think that *I* should be the one helping Mr. White find Johnny...and not you" she announced. Wendy rubbed her eyes in a tired expression, feeling fed up with the conversation.

"I don't think you should help him. You don't know what I *saw,* Christine. What Johnny truly *looked* like. It was...horrifying" she said, muttering her last few words in shaken lips. Some tears were coming now, and she didn't have enough strength to hold them back. Christine came over to her with a comforting embrace. Wendy quietly whimpered in her sister's arms, and gently moved out of them.

"I'm going to bed now. I feel like...my life is changed forever...and I just want to sleep" she declared. She hobbled toward her bedroom door, relishing the fact that her home was all on the same floor and no staircase would pose a challenge for her. She truly *did* feel like her life would never be the same now, and maybe after sleeping it would all just be a dream. A foolish thought, but one that was wishful thinking. Christine watched her sister leave and she heard the sound of the wind pick up again around the house. Rattling the windows and rumbling the walls. She'd already decided on what she must do, and that was to go see Johnny, herself. She remembered where the road was that the trucker had found Wendy's wrecked station wagon two years ago. Just outside of Roswell, maybe an hour away. She would simply follow it and attempt to discover if Wendy's memories were real...or just all in her head.

Chapter 14

The solid sound of knocking woke Wendy from a deep sleep as her eyes opened slowly. The soft pale blue light of the morning, fading into white poked between her eyelids from her bedroom window as her mind rose from slumber. It passed through the curtains with a genial glow. At first, she thought she was dreaming the sound, but it came again, and this time it was louder than before. She discovered it was coming from the front door, and no one was answering it. Peering over at the tiny alarm clock she kept beside her bed on the nightstand, she realized it was only just after six am. She wondered who in their right mind would be knocking on her door at this hour. Hopefully not one of those persistent traveling salesmen wanting to show off a new vacuum at the break of dawn. By this time, the dust storm had long passed sometime in the middle of the night, and Christine was probably dead asleep. Wendy would have to answer the door now since she'd heard it first. Something she really didn't feel like doing upon waking up. She'd rather have coffee, but her curiosity was fueling her to stand up with her crutch and walk awkwardly into the living room in her nightgown. Her hair fell down partly out of the tie she placed it in before sleeping, due to her movements in her sleep, and noticed Christine's bedroom door was still shut. Obviously, she didn't hear the knocking then.

A shadow loomed just beyond the tinted glass of the front door, indicating someone was waiting to be answered. Wendy cautiously opened it, and to her relief...and somewhat surprise...she found a familiar handsome face. He was dressed in rugged blue jeans, with a white tank top as his long and elegant black hair draped down around his shoulders, chest, and his back. He too, looked as though he'd woken up not very long ago, but *his* hair was well combed and ready for the day. Maybe he was an early riser since working on the farm he lived on. His hazelnut colored eyes gleamed at her kindly, but no smile was on his lips. In fact, he seemed to be quite alert and worried.

"Mohan?..." Wendy said weakly, shielding her eyes from the rising sun. The young man stepped forward slightly at the sound of his name to greet her. Just the way the sunlight glazed his caramel skin tone, made him look like a morning angel come to see her. He was beautiful like a dream, and Wendy felt herself beginning to smile already.

"Hello, Miss Wendy" was all he said at first. His head tilted again at the sight of her, just like before…and again, it reminded her of a cat. He blinked at her appearance, and realized he'd woken her by mistake. "I'm very sorry to wake you" he spoke again, feeling apologetic. His voice was very soft and entered Wendy's ears in delicate fashion. She straightened her hair up quickly to better her appearance for him, and spoke clearer this time.

"What brings you here?" she asked him. If he were anyone else, Wendy would've surely been much more upset about the knocking so early in the morning. She genuinely wanted to see this man again, no matter what time of day. She only wished she'd looked better in this moment.

"I…feel very worried" Mohan said then, bringing his hands together without a sound. He held them up just below his chin in a child-like fashion. "I feel something may be very wrong with you and Miss Christine" he admitted. Wendy's eyes narrowed at Mohan's curious words, but then slowly became wide as he knew what he was trying to say. Mohan had been lured here by his instinct, feeling something had been very wrong and dangerous. She immediately turned and hobbled over to Christine's room. She flung open the door, and saw no one inside. Mohan invited himself in and came up behind Wendy. He was just as concerned as she was in this moment, and he only hoped he'd be wrong about the feeling that woke him, but soon discovered his suspicion was correct. A note was lying on Christine's bed in the room. The words seemed to be written quickly, and Wendy knew her sister had left the house sometime in the night. Probably when the storm was gone.

Wendy,

I went to look for the diner you told me about and see if it's there or not. I don't know if I will find Johnny, but I will tell you if I do. Please don't be angry, I'm only trying to keep you safe. I will be back home later and we'll have pizza together.

Love, Christine

"She has gone to find him...the shadow creature from the other world" Mohan explained. Wendy dropped the note on the floor and brought her hands up to her face. She felt it was all her fault, and Christine was now in danger. She would have to go there again...to the Moonbeam Diner...and see *him* again. The monster known as Johnny. Mohan placed a hand on Wendy's shoulder in comfort, and Wendy turned to face him. Her eyes held a sense of determination and boldness, as well as tiny tears swelling inside them. He wasn't expecting this reaction from her.

"We have to stop her" Wendy told him. "And I need your help...before Johnny gets to her." She wiped the tears away, trying to hold them back. Finding a sense of bravery was something she needed right now, for she felt if she didn't have it, then Christine may never come home safely. She would most likely be devoured by Johnny and then Wendy would've failed to save her only living relative. Christine couldn't fathom just how much of foolish decision she made. Wendy and Mohan were her only hope now.

Mohan nodded gently in agreement, and he took her by the hand. He knew he was the only person now who could possibly help, and police would be of no use. The elusive Mr. White was nowhere to be found, and had never given them a way to contact him. Perhaps he would be stalking Wendy before hand and follow them to the diner, but for now he was unreliable.

"I promise to protect you, Miss Wendy" Mohan told her kindly. He still didn't smile, but his sincere expression was enough to let her know that she could rely on him for help. She wouldn't have to go alone. Not this time. He was here with her, and it gave her a sense of confidence that she hoped she could hold onto once she saw Johnny again. She truly had no idea how her mind and body would react upon the sight of this atrocious being, but one thing Johnny was going to realize, is humans can find courage even in the darkest of times.

Chapter 15

    Even in the morning, the heat of the sun is relentless in the western sky. The fiery circle loomed over the horizon behind them as it lit up the long stretch of land down the road. Wendy gazed out the passenger window of Mohan's truck as they rode along in the same direction she did that one night.

The night when everything changed.

Her mind had many racing thoughts. She couldn't seem to focus them. What felt like a noble decision back at the house to go and find Christine, was now being overwhelmed with paranoia. Staring into the vastness of the rocky desert made the world feel much larger than what it was in Roswell. Out here...she was vulnerable. Anything could happen. Even the road ahead of them was unpredicted. She didn't know if the fogbank would still be there or not. By this time, she had a pretty good feeling it wasn't truly a real cloud of fog…but merely the entrance to another world. She'd given this plenty of thought over time. Maybe it was Johnny's doorway into his crafted version of Hell, and people didn't know because it looked like the world they currently lived in. It was an illusion to distract people from the truth. She remembered how different things looked once she passed through the fog before. She remembered how much brighter the stars were, and how the diner itself didn't feel quite normal. Maybe there was only one explanation for it.

Johnny was from another dimension.

It almost all made sense now. Mohan said before, the creature was from another world that was close to their own. Either he meant that Johnny was from another planet…or a being from another dimension, opposite everyone else's world. Even Mr. White once said *"I'm the same as him"* when referring to what Johnny really is, and *"I'm not what you would call an alien"* when referring to himself. If Mr. White and Johnny were the same kind of being, then they're also from the same dimension. They were aliens, but not the kind from outer space. Unless of course…they came from another planet…while in another dimension. Anything was possible now. Roswell wasn't without its share of alien-talk, that's for sure. Its recent history had many stories to tell, and it was bringing in visitors far and wide to hear about them. Some of the townsfolk called them "outsiders". Wendy would believe in all of them now. Who is truly to say...whether or not she went into another dimension? People think everything is just a *story* until they experience it for themselves. It's the same for extraterrestrials from other worlds. It would be foolish to think we're the *only* species to ever inhabit the *entire* ocean of space. The universe is just too massive to be completely empty. That would be...a waste of space.

    Wendy turned her eyes over to Mohan beside her in the truck. They'd been riding together for almost twenty to thirty minutes now on the route from Roswell heading toward Arizona. Mohan's truck was a beige colored '59 Chevrolet Apache, and without air conditioning. The windows were rolled down for a breezeway of air between them, but the heat still made a heavy presence. Mohan didn't seem to mind it though, and in fact, he looked quite comfortable. He drove his truck with merely one hand, and sat sluggishly like a teen boy, resting his elbow on the window sill beside him. His long black hair blowing wildly in the wind. He hadn't spoken much since leaving town, but he seemed to know the way where Wendy had been before. This road didn't have many side roads, and he seemed to have traveled on it in the past. It was true, Wendy didn't know much about this man, but still felt that she could trust him.

"Mohan?" Wendy caught his attention, speaking his name loud enough above the sound of the roaring wind.

"Yes, Miss Wendy?" he answered with his own question. He glanced at her quickly, letting her know he'd heard her voice but then focused on the road again. She was almost hesitant to ask him this, but figured he was one with an open mind to begin with. Otherwise they wouldn't be in this situation together.

"Do you…believe in aliens?" she asked him. It was a direct question, even if she hesitated. Something in her mind had to know what he believed. It would give her reassurance. Mohan sat up a bit in his seat, but still managed to look relaxed. His reply came without looking at the woman, but he seemed sure of himself.

"I believe in many kinds beings…and some of them are not of this world. I believe in many kinds of worlds too. Worlds far beyond our sky...and worlds that are hidden all around us" he answered. His genial and somewhat vague response gave Wendy exactly what she needed to know. Reassurance...that she was not the only one to believe. Mohan made her feel comfortable. He made her feel like she could tell him anything, and he wouldn't laugh at it. No matter how outrageous it would seem to most people. *He* would understand her.

"I think the question is...what do *you* believe, Miss Wendy?" Mohan asked her gently. His kind voice made his question easy to answer, and Wendy found herself smiling at him.

"I believe in them too, Mohan. I believe in everything that *you* do. Our world is just too complex, not to hold any mysteries about it. Life has never made complete sense to me, and I've always felt there was more to it. *Much* more to it" she told him. Never before, had she felt so confident in saying this to anyone. It was a relief, and her mind felt calmer now. She was still dreading the impending situation, but she was glad that she and Mohan had the same thoughts. It made him that much more reliable and trustworthy.

Sitting up in his truck completely now, Mohan slowly applied the break as the speedometer when from sixty down to a crawling movement. They came to a stop in the center of the left lane on the road, and the two of them stared ahead at what appeared to be the fogbank. It was massive in size, and it made Wendy realize she had never truly seen just how large it was until now. It blocked the entire horizon in front of them as it drifted over the road. It looked like a large grayish-black storm cloud floating over the land, and it was swirling in casual fashion as if it were alive. It didn't look natural at all. Wendy had caught her breath and held it for nearly a minute, along with Mohan. No cars were coming behind them, so it was merely just the two of them alone on the road together. They had no idea what would be ahead of them beyond this colossal cloud. It was so thick and obscuring, they couldn't see anything through it.

"I wonder…why no one has mentioned this" Mohan spoke out, feeling mesmerized by the immense presence of the cloud. Wendy said the first thing that came to her mind, and it made the most sense in their current situation.

"Because everyone who's seen it…never comes back out again" she answered. The two of them turned and looked at each other with almost the same expression on their faces. One of uncertainty, fear and curiosity. Mohan knew about this entrance to another world, but it was clear that he hadn't approached it nor gone through it on his own. This would be his first time.

"No one has come out of it...except for *you*" he said to her. It was surely the reason why Johnny wanted her so badly; because she'd been the only meal he never got to taste. She had a sudden memory of the trucker who saved her life after she nearly smashed her station wagon into him the day she ran from Johnny. He too, would've most likely been devoured by Johnny's drooling fangs if she hadn't wrecked on the road. The most unusual part about that, however, is the fact that Wendy made it back to Roswell again while in a coma. Christine had gone to Roswell too. Surely they would've had to go through the cloud again, right? Unless...after wounding Johnny...the fog had temporarily disappeared. As though he controlled when he made it appear in the human world. This would mean that Johnny was no longer in any pain. He was hungry again, and waiting for unsuspecting prey to wander into his lair.

"It reminds me of The Blob" Wendy said right then, staring at the fogbank from where she sat. Mohan cocked his head in confusion as he looked at his friend. "The...*blob*?" he asked her. He didn't quite know why she said this, or even *what* she was referencing. Wendy pushed her glasses back up to her face as they slide down her nose.

"Sorry...I guess you never seen that movie" she said to him. It was honestly the first thing they hadn't connected on since knowing each other. Mohan smiled in embarrassment, and turned back to the road again.

"Ah, yes...I don't go to the cinema much" he admitted. "But it's always interested me. Perhaps you and I can see this blob you speak of together one day."

Wendy couldn't help but smile at him in return, and gave a slow nod in agreement. She reached over and held Mohan's hand. She felt that he probably didn't have very many friends, if any at all, or connected with people very often. Him, and his father were probably loner cactus farmers outside of Roswell, not bothering to talk with people much. In all honesty, Wendy had done the same thing for years after her mother died. She'd only gone to work every day, and then gone home. Rarely had she gone out anywhere in town. Thinking about her job, she wondered what she would do for income in the future. It was long ago that she was informed about her position being replaced after falling into a coma. She couldn't blame her former boss for doing so, since it was unpredicted whether or not she would recover. It's not like she enjoyed the job very much anyway. It was merely a way to make ends meet at the time. Meeting this young man beside her was the first positive thing to happen to her since reentering the world again. She was completely happy to form a friendship with him.

"Yeah...maybe we will, Mohan" she replied in a comforting tone. He then made the truck move forward again as they advanced into the fog. Ready or not, they were going into Johnny's world. Christine was still lost inside, and they only hoped she wouldn't be in pieces once they found her again.

Chapter 16

The murky mass of deep fog shrouded them quickly, even as Mohan drove slowly. The light of the day was gone completely in under a minute when they entered the misty cloud. It was so thick immediately, and the air dropped in temperature in a very abnormal way. The sweat on Wendy and Mohan's body felt the coolness first, and they both soon rolled up their windows to shield themselves. After all, who knows what truly was inside this fog. Even while dreading the appearance of the Moonbeam Diner, it was possible they would see other things in here as well. Nothing was certain.

The air was beginning to freeze around the body of Mohan's truck now. The ice formed across the window, and the engine started to jerk a bit. Mohan's first reaction was to go slower, but Wendy held his arm and directed him quickly.

"No…go faster. Otherwise it might stall" she told him. "I remember this." Her eyes were serious and Mohan listened to her without questioning, and applied speed while the truck could still move. The icicles were growing faster as they zoomed through the mass, but they needed to get through it or they would never see the other side. Being trapped in here would be a terrible fate. They would certainly freeze to death. The truck gave another lurch as it struggled, but Mohan stepped harder on the gas pedal. They reached nearly eighty miles per hour until the daylight soon peeked through ahead of them. Wendy had been holding her breath and she let out a gasp of relief. Slowing down the vehicle once more, Mohan cautiously rubbed Wendy's hand to help calm her again.

"It's alright now, Miss Wendy" he said to her gently. "We made it through."

It was amazing how the heat of the sun was back again so quickly. Already, the two of them could feel the beam shining through the windshield. It was melting the ice at an alarming rate. They were here now…in Johnny's world. Wendy already recognized it, but she felt it was different than before. Probably because she'd never been here during the daytime. She did remember how the dawn was rising during the moment she ran from Johnny the last time, but the sun was much brighter the second time being here. The clock on the truck's dashboard was stopped completely. It'd been around 10 am when they first entered the fog, but now the clock ceased to move. Either time was frozen in this world, or it worked differently from the human world. The clock had stopped the exact moment they passed through the entrance of this world.

"Look ahead" Mohan spoke up, staring at the road in front of them. His eyes grew larger and more focused. He was much more alert than before. Wendy turned and seen two things ahead of them. The first thing, was the bright yellow Mercury that Christine had rented the day before. It was sitting in the middle of the road, sidelong over both lanes as the driver's side faced them. The door was left open and smoke from the exhaust was puffing out the tailpipe. The car was still running…with no one inside of it. Christine was surely here now, but must have been distracted enough to leave the car in such a careless position. It looked like Christine had been in the process of turning the car around to leave the area, but then stopped and left it there indefinitely.

The second thing that Wendy saw...was the diner. It was on the right side of the road, just like she remembered, and shining brightly in the light. The sun reflected off of the long and rectangular chrome box sitting in the desert quietly. The very presence of this building was loud, even thought it didn't make a sound. It was loud in the sense that it captured your attention, and never let it go once it had you. This was obviously the reason why Christine left the Mercury running in the roadway. She'd been so distracted by the sight of this place, that she couldn't focus on anything else. It'd been that way for Wendy too, the same night she first came here. Although, the neon turquoise blue lighting wasn't lit. The same display sign on the tall pole was standing again. The rocket ship symbol sailing passed the crescent moon shape with the fancy lettering saying *"Moonbeam Diner"* below it. She remembered how her wagon had backed into it during a fleeting panic, and knocked it over. Johnny must've repaired it since then. Probably to keep up the illusion and welcome more travelers for his greedy consumption.

Wendy thoughts began to race now. She felt her head becoming heavy as a wave of dizziness struck her almost instantly. She clutched the sides of her head and gasped loudly for air as visions soared through her mind. Her glasses fell on her lap and Mohan threw his arms around her to stop her from falling forward. She saw herself crawling on the floor of the diner again, and Johnny's hungry arms scraping the tiles and he reached for her. He tore up the floor with his jagged fingers, that didn't form any nails, but rather long and sharp pointed ends in his solid black skin. His long dripping fangs pierced deep into her flesh as he bit into her, sending jets of her blood into the open air as she screamed. He was trying to get to her. He knew she was close now…and he was trying to tease her by entering her thoughts. She felt his powerful energy pressing against her body. It was like being strangled by fire as it burned the air around her. The feeling of a thousand needles all stabbing into her flesh at once. Mohan shook Wendy's body forcefully as she finally came out of the vision. She immediately wrapped her arms around the man and began to cry uncontrollably. He held her close to him and softly stroked her back as she tried to catch her breath.

"It's okay Wendy…I'm here with you. He's not going to hurt you. Not while I'm here" he reassured her. His genial voice was direct and protective now. His beautiful brown eyes, now serious and dominating. Wendy was safe with him, and somehow Johnny knew this. She could sense it in her mind. His energy backed off when he sensed Mohan's aura. He had a certain protection surrounding him, and it made Johnny angry. He would most likely do whatever he could in order to get to her now. The very fact that Christine was here felt more like a lure to bring Wendy in, rather than a mission to stop her from certain death. Maybe Johnny had tricked Christine into coming here, because he knew Wendy would follow her back here. No one knew for sure, but it was the thought Wendy was having now. By invading her dreams and thoughts, Johnny may have tried to lure Wendy back unsuccessfully. Christine was his only option left. Johnny was a trickster by nature who was probably used to getting what he wanted, and would go about any means necessary to accomplish his goals. He was a selfish being who didn't like his prey running away from him. Wendy was probably the first human to ever give him such a "problem".

She found it easier to gather herself when Mohan's strong arms held her close to him. His aura was the most comforting experience she'd ever felt. It was amazing how quickly and softly it calmed her entire body. There was something about this man that was unlike anything else. Every time she thought about him or looked at him, it was a very distinct and extraordinary energy that made them link together. Maybe it was just his way of calming anyone around him. He was a healer, and a messenger of truth and wisdom.

"I'm so scared of going inside there" she mumbled to him weakly. Mohan leaned her up again and looked into worried eyes with his own. He made a delicate smile to help her relax.

"He will try to harm you, Wendy...but I won't let him. I promise that" he assured her. His eyes told her the truth. He never looked away from her. For anyone else, it was most likely a promise they couldn't keep, but for him it seemed believable. She didn't know what Mohan planned to do once Johnny showed himself, because they came here unarmed. All she could do was trust in his words.

Stepping out into the blazing sun, the heat from the light made Wendy shield her eyes as they approached the yellow Mercury ahead of them. She rested against the car after limping over with her crutch, and Mohan turned off the engine. He looked at the fuel gage and seen it was nearly empty now. If they'd arrived here any later, the car would've run out of gas on its own. This also meant that no other visitors had been here for hours as well, since they would've seen the car and stopped. No other vehicles sat in the parking lot of the diner.

"It's been running for a while now. The creature is keeping her inside there" he said, referring to Christine. Wendy was staring at the diner with a cautious look and holding her hands together tightly in front of herself. The windows of the chromed eatery were so reflective that she couldn't see inside. It made the building look even more fake during the day, and they heard the distant humming sound the diner always made. It vibrated over the ground and she could feel it in the earth below the asphalt of the road. Mohan felt it too, and it reminded them that they were standing in the presence of something powerful and unnatural. Wendy knew the diner itself was just an illusion, or even just a façade to lure in Johnny's victims. It was where he lived in this world. He'd placed here, right near the borderline between his world and the human world for easy access to his meals. In reality, he was following his instincts, but doing so in a very selfish and murderous way. She couldn't help but still remember Mr. White telling her about him being the same kind of creature, and how *he* didn't eat humans, unlike Johnny did. It gave her the notion that Johnny didn't require the taste of human flesh to be alive...he just *preferred* it over anything else. Wendy still couldn't quite grasp the fact that she was standing in another world in this moment. One that felt very close to her own, but clearly had its differences. She wanted to leave, but she wanted Christine back home with her.

"He's waiting for us" she said allowed, without looking away from the building. Mohan walked up beside her and took her by the hand again.

"Yes...he is. Stay close to me, Wendy. We don't know when he will strike...and he his movements will be quick" he replied, informatively. The way Mohan spoke about him, made it seem like they were hunting down some sort of animal, but it made sense. Johnny wasn't human, and he had a voracious display of behavior, so they could refer to him as an animal. One that could plot, speak, and tear them apart. Onc that could disguise himself to hunt successfully. He was like a spider, setting a trap and waiting for prey to fall into it.

Chapter 17

Mohan lead the way by walking slightly ahead of Wendy. He continued to hold her hand for added support as she hobbled along. He felt the strong vibration of the building when the touched the chromed handles of the front doors, and pulled them open vigilantly.

Peeking inside the room, he seen the lights were brightly lit and showing off the blue and white tiled design that Wendy first seen two years ago. In fact, she was now standing in the room with Mohan just beyond the front doors as they closed behind them. She knew there was no use in trying to open them again. Johnny had them locked in place just like before. Once you entered the inviting diner, there was no going back out. A steady hum of neon could be heard around them, and everything looked just as clean and spotless as it did the first time. Mohan shifted his eyes slowly around the room, hoping to catch a glimpse of their target in question, but nothing made a sound. No movement could be seen, and nothing out of the ordinary.

"It looks the same as before...nothing has changed" Wendy observed. Mohan quickly brought a finger up to his lips, and shushed his friend quietly.

"He's listening..." was all he said. Wendy silenced herself in time to hear a tranquil melody start up in the room. Immediately turning their heads toward the jukebox at the right side of the diner, a song drifted through the air and cradled around their bodies like a welcoming friend. It was *"Johnny Angel"* sung by Shelley Fabares. Wendy recognized it by the way the song starts, and repeating the words of the title over and over until the main sequence started. The singer's elegant voice flooded the room, seeping into every nook and cranny. Wendy narrowed her eyes and turned away from the music with a disgusted expression.

How very fitting. She thought to herself in sarcasm.

She knew it was Johnny's way of announcing his own presence. The last time it was *"Sleep Walk"* that played continuously before, but that was after he'd already done his introductions. Mohan stared ahead toward the kitchen doors and Wendy felt his arm gently push her back behind him in a protective action. He began to shield her from something and she peered around him to see what it was. She turned her eyes in the same direction to find the suave and grinning Johnny standing against wall...leaning there like a sassy teen boy, and folding arms as his fluffy blonde hair fell to one side of his face. His piercing eyes glowed brighter than the ceiling lamps in the room, and he seemed very sure of himself upon discovering his new company. He's always delighted in seeing new visitors. He held one foot propped against the wall behind him, and he slowly cocked his head before speaking.

"Weeennndyyy..." he breathed out in a humming articulation that whispered higher than the sound of the music. "...I have missed you." His eyes flashed at her as she backed against the wall. Her mind wanted to scream, but no sound came from her lips. It was *him.* The creature she'd been dreading to see all this time. He'd surprised them by popping out from nowhere, and was quick to greet them. She could almost see the heat of his breath when she spoke, drifting delicately around the sharpened ends of his protruding fangs. His lips curled around them as he showed them off. His wicked grin tickling at her senses as her skin began to crawl at the mere sight of them. His teeth were perfectly white as his tongue bathed them with his saliva. He stroked them lovingly as he stared at the new person in the room.

"My, *my*...what have we here? You brought a rather *delicious* looking young man along with you, Wendy" he observed with hungry eyes. His voice danced through the room in a slow and enticing manner, as graceful as the tune floating around them. Mohan focused his angry expression at the creature when Johnny made a soft kissy face at him. A quick pucker of his tender pink lips just to tease him. The creature's pale skin, imitating that of human's quickly blushed in light red around his cheeks. "I would really *love* to lick...every inch...of that body." Johnny confessed, in a very flirtatious and lustful way. "Don't be shy...I know you like me too. You and I could have some fun before I feed."

Mohan was aghast by the foulness in behavior that Johnny was displaying. It was true that he could feel the energy that Johnny was forcing over him, and he felt a slight sexual attraction to it. He was trying his hardest to lure him in with a sense of lust, just like he'd done with Wendy. He probably had done this with all of his victims, no matter male or female. However, what Johnny didn't understand, was that Mohan's willpower was stronger, and his energy would overpower the creature's alluring state faster than he expected.

Stepping forward without taking his eyes away from him, Mohan's once caring and beautiful face was now serious and dominating. His kind eyes were in full alert and cruel in appearance. He clearly despised this creature in front of him, and refused to be phased by his lustful intentions. Wendy slid away against the wall to further herself from the two of them, as it seemed Mohan was taking control of the situation. The young Native American man was impressively brave as he walked close to Johnny. The only thing that separated the two from each other was the chromed countertop of the room. Johnny smiled at him playfully, and lightly let his tongue seep out between his fangs and lips as he spoke to him.

"Care for a kiss?" he asked him. Again, Mohan stood completely still and domineering. His eyes never moved as Johnny's tongue extended closer to him above the counter far longer than any human's could. Drops of his sticky saliva fell in tiny drip sounds over the counter's top surface. To the creature's sudden surprise, the swift motion of Mohan's hand gripped the slimy black colored tongue in a tight fist. It stopped Johnny's movements as Mohan locked him there, and Johnny screamed in pain as he felt the man rip his tongue completely out of his mouth in one short pull. Mohan did so without moving his body, and only one arm. The strength of that arm displaying his brutal force and uncaring feelings for him, as Johnny scrambled away from him. The panicking creature fell back against the wall like a flopping fish out of water, clutching his mouth in a show of gushing dark red blood spewing down around his neck. Mohan dropped the tongue to the floor, where it slowly melted into thick black goo and oozed its way back to its owner. The jelly-like mass curled itself around Johnny's foot and slowly merged with it unnaturally. Johnny's bright eyes held a sense of apologetic fear, and also sudden anger toward this man for his vicious attack.

"How *dare* you..." he growled at him, letting tiny blood bubbles gurgle out of his mouth when he spoke. Clearly, still wounded and in pain. The seeping blood was slowing now, and Johnny seemed to be closing the wound rapidly with some sort of regenerative ability. It would certainly explain why he healed over time after being struck by Wendy's car before. Mohan said nothing in response to the creature's anger, and Wendy stopped moving at the sight of the scene unfolding in front of her. She held her breath in surprise at what she witnessed, realizing just how strong Mohan truly was. He was either crazy to attack Johnny with no other means of protection, or blinded by the fury of keeping her safe and destroying this menacing alien. It was true, she didn't know everything about Mohan, but she was shocked at such a bold move coming from his delicate demeanor.

"Your persuasive powers are strong...but they are *not* stronger than my will" Mohan affirmed, staring at Johnny with immense hatred. His eyes were fearsome and dominating as Johnny looked at him. He stood up again completely in a sluggish manner, as if worried he'd be assaulted again and whimpered softly in return. He flinched even at the sound of his own unnatural voice.

"H-How...c-could...y-you?!" he exclaimed, forming small tears in his fake blue eyes. "I really liked you...we've could've had fun together!"

Mohan's face never changed as he listened to Johnny's pitiful statement. He knew he was no longer feeling any physical pain, and only felt a hurt sense of pride that he'd let a mere human attack him so easily. Wendy slowly brought her arms up to her mouth as she watched Mohan do something *very* unnatural and sudden. The man gently raised his arms to waist length, and several of the chairs surrounding the counter began to rise with them in midair. They floated aimlessly around Mohan's body and soon began to swirl around him in a constant circle. They never touched him as a breeze formed in the room from the motion, and his hair became aloft in the wind. They rotated continuously around, gaining speed as Mohan narrowed his brows at Johnny. Wendy didn't understand what she was witnessing...but it seemed to her, that Mohan was controlling the flying chairs with his mind. The only thing she could compare it to, was a phenomenon called *Telekinesis.* She'd once read about it in a book based on Parapsychology, which suggested that few humans had the ability to harness the power of the invisible energy surrounding all objects and people. Their minds are then able to manipulate it into moving anything without physical force. Clearly...Mohan had a secret about him...and he'd just revealed it to the world.

"You are a foul creature...and one that should be destroyed, rather than let you slay others for selfish gain" Mohan's voice declared darkly at Johnny, whom was now watching this human in awe from what he was doing. The look of the flying chairs around this man made Johnny nervous and his panic returned quickly. He soon realized this was no ordinary human, and he was one that would put up a fight if he tried to consume him.

"What are you doing?!" he questioned in fear, shifting his eyes back and forth as the room of the diner soon began to vibrate. The countertop rumbled between them and the floor moaned from a constant tension as Mohan's mind soon connected with everything around him. The deafening sound of the plates and silverware on the tables shaking and falling to the floor in shattering pieces made Wendy cover her ears quickly. The chairs were now moving so fast; they no longer resembled anything but a mass of motion around Mohan's body. The wind blew around the room like a fan and Johnny raised his arms up to shield himself. His long and drippy black tentacles slithered their way out of his back again from under his false clothing, extending four more arms to help protect himself. He was entering an animalistic defense mode while preparing his body from impending danger. "What kind of human are you?! Answer me!" he cried out once more. Mohan's eyes opened as he replied to the creature's plea.

"One that is stronger than *you!*" his voice dominated over him, sending the flying chairs directly into Johnny's body as a splash of the creature's blood spewed into the air. Johnny let out a certain inhuman scream that Wendy's ears would never forget. The force of the collision pushed him through the wall and into the kitchen behind him. The chromed door followed him inward and fell on top of his body. Wendy collapsed to the floor as Mohan continued his assault. Johnny rose from the rubble, fully reanimated into his natural form, melting any fake skin he used for disguise into his own darkened exterior. The creature's skin was completely black in color…so black that the light of the room reflected off it like a mirror and Mohan could see his own face on the being's body. He walked up to Johnny whom was now growling in defense like an obscuring dog, and he quickly slithered away from him around his legs and back out into the dining area where Wendy was. She saw the creature coming straight toward her and his mouth opening wide with rows of jagged fangs pointed at her. Johnny was attempting to devour her before Mohan could stop him, in a way of revenge more so than nourishment. Wendy's scream caught

Mohan's attention as she covered her face in panic. It was the most horrifying sight she'd ever seen, and was sure she was about to meet her final end when Johnny's body quickly revolted and flinched in severe pain. Mohan lifted several of the kitchen's knives and meat cleavers as he sent them jetting down into the creature's body from afar. His arsenal of weapons was all around them in the building, as he could literally use anything to stop him from moving. Johnny crawled away down the left side row of the diner and removed the knives from his dark skin. Each of them falling on the tiles in loud metal clinks and clangs. The sight of the blood dripping and gushing on the floor made Wendy sick to her stomach, and her tears streamed down her face. She covered her eyes, but couldn't block everything from her sight. Too much sound and movements were happing in the room, and she couldn't do anything but sit there and try to shield herself from danger. She had to keep in mind that Mohan was protecting her. He would stop Johnny by any means necessary, and she knew she must wait until this was over and done with. Johnny would never stop hunting her until Mohan killed him. This is why they came here. She had to remind herself of this, or she would surely go insane from this experience.

Mohan stood in the middle of the dining room now, with Johnny standing at the left end of the row and facing him with piercing red eyes deep within his black and gooey surface. There was no longer any resemblance of the attractive Johnny that Wendy remembered, and this creature could no longer hide himself from them. Every time he tried to transform again, Mohan would stop him with another protruding object into his body and wounding him. It would stop him from attempting to disguise and trick him, and Mohan knew he must keep attacking or this thing may escape the scene.

"I *devoured* her, you know!" Johnny said in a guttural tone as he glared wildly at Mohan with his drooling rows of large teeth. He was back to taunting him again, and making a confession. "Wendy's sister made an *excellent* meal as I waited for you both to come here!" he exclaimed. Wendy soon began to sob uncontrollably at the sound of the creature's words, and she fell to the floor, holding her arms around her body in agony of losing her only family. Mohan raised his brows with widened eyes, and somehow they both knew this alien being was telling the truth. After all, Christine was nowhere to be found, and nor did they find any evidence that she'd survived. It was possible the creature was lying, just to get them angry, but he was already being attacked. What good would it do to suddenly lie to them about eating Christine? He *had* to be telling the truth...and this truth made Mohan even angrier than before. He wasn't about to let this useless creature taunt him any further. He was here to kill him, and stop his murderous ways of innocent people from the human world. He was here to protect Wendy, his only friend. Mohan was the only person with the power to do so, and he would keep attacking Johnny until the world around them ended if he needed to. He knew the creature was confessing now, because Mohan was stronger and making him panic. He was trying to be menacing again, and failing to scare anyone except for Wendy.

Johnny raised his long tentacles high into the air, as several tiny mouths began to show themselves on the ends of the pods. Each of them ready to tear apart Mohan and Wendy's bodies for an easier meal to his liking. The front of the jukebox at the right side of the room shattered as the glass fell around the soundboard. The vinyl records rose out of the machine and began to ship themselves toward the creature viciously through the air. Each one, cutting deeply into Johnny's skin and making him scream when they broke under his skin. Their jagged edges pierced into him in several locations. Wendy watched the tentacles falling on the floor, and their tiny mouths crying out for their loss of movement, and beginning to melt over the tiles. The records sliced Johnny's body quickly, soon followed by the entire machine vaulting through the air as it struck the creature's body with a thunderous sound. The music box pushed him down on the floor with a splash of Johnny's blood and black goo spraying everywhere inside the room. Wendy could feel the collision shake the floor violently as Mohan lodged the machine upon his victim. The windows of the diner all shattered in a violent storm of glass and metal. The beams of the chromed ceiling bent themselves down over Johnny, and lunged themselves into his body. Quickly walking up to the creature, Mohan raised his hands over the alien in the air and held them there indefinitely. Johnny felt the force of Mohan's mind pressing down upon him, and holding him in place. He could no longer move, nor regenerate completely with Mohan keeping him under his control. Johnny whimpered again, but spoke in a growling tone as one of his eyeballs slowly slid out of its gooey socket upon looking up his attacker.

"Let…me…go…" he mumbled out to him, feeling angry in his defeat. For all the years that Johnny had been stalking and slaying people, he'd never once met one that could overpower him. Mohan was truly unique, and possibly the only person in the world who could stop him.

"You don't deserve to live" Mohan said calmingly, glaring down at his victim without remorse. Wendy soon watched a pair of black shoes walk by her on the tiled floor. They barely made a noise as they quietly approached the scene, and moving toward Mohan and the creature. Her eyes looked upward at the sight of a man in a black suit and fedora hat walking in the room. He almost seemed to be moving in slow motion, but she knew it was only her own eyesight feeling strained from the wind that'd blown around beforehand. It was Mr. White. She was sure of it. The man slowly approached Johnny with a type of weapon in his hand. A shiny metal gun that was silvery in appearance with an abnormal design. She couldn't quite make it out from where she laid on the floor, but she could tell it was nothing that humans had ever produced in her world. Mr. White raised the gun and pointed it directly at the wounded creature pinned on the floor under the damaged jukebox. Mohan continued to hold him in place with his mind, and the suited man spoke clearly through the silence.

"I'll take it from here, Mohan. I thank you for your assistance" he said directly. He was sure of his words, and waited for Mohan's hands to move away before aiming the gun at Johnny's head. The creature spoke one last time before Mr. White pulled the trigger, and he replied in return with a stoic expression.

"I'm not the only one...there will be other's like me. Do you feel...accomplished?" Johnny gargled at the men above him. His eyeball had long since rolled out into the thick mess of his body melting around him. He slowly formed a small grin at the man, and could see himself in the reflection of his dark sunglasses.

"I know. That's why I'm here...and yes...I feel accomplished in ridding this world of your ghastly presence" was the reply of the mysterious Mr. White, and he pulled the trigger of his gun. A beam of hot red light shot out from the tip quickly and it melted Johnny's remains into a bubbling mass that slowly cooked away into nothing. The smoke rising from the heat began to fill the room quickly, along with a nauseating smell that churned Wendy's stomach. The last sounds of Johnny's screams would forever haunt her memories as she turned away in disgust. Her eyes refused to open, and she soon felt the arms of

Mohan scoop her up from the floor. He lifted her delicately in his grasp, and leaned her body into his own. Her eyes reminded shut until the sunlight of the outdoors touched her face with a comforting warmness. Opening them again, she saw the outside of the crumpled diner...and several black cars lined up in the parking lot in front of them. Mohan stood there heroically; holding his friend in his strong protective arms as Mr. White walked passed them. He turned back, and spoke to them before leaving the scene in his dark colored Edsel.

"You're free now, Miss Fields. May we never have to meet again the future" he said to her in a calm tone, but one that was serious and direct. "I'm dreadfully sorry...for the loss of your sister. It is certain the creature devoured her, just as he admitted to doing so."

Wendy's tears fell from her face as she lay in Mohan's grasp like a child. She truly did feel helpless and needy, and she nodded to Mr. White in return. Several men were standing around them in the area, all under Mr. White's command. The man gave a wave of his fingers to them, and they all quickly rushed into the diner to clean up the scene and investigate the years of Johnny's killings. Mohan looked down at Wendy as her eyes met up with his. Gently, he smiled at her and leaned down to touch his lips on her forehead. The sweet gesture gave Wendy reassurance that she was safe with him. Where they would go from here was uncertain, and he slowly made his way back to the truck they came here in. Wendy looked down the road for the fog, and realized it'd been lifted. Probably due to the fact that Johnny was now dead. The world around them seemed more realistic now too, and they got the notion that they were now back in the world of human life. Mr. White's men were busy closing off the scene of the Moonbeam Diner, which would soon be dismantled and torn down. The location would be smoothed away and left deserted in the rocky land around it. No evidence to show that anything had happened there. Wendy would go home again, living the remainder of her life in Roswell, or wherever she decided to be. She mourned the loss of her sister deeply, and would hold a funeral for her with the help of Mohan. Even if Christine's body was no longer a physical thing. Maybe she would live with Mohan on his farm, along with his father. Only time would tell the tale. She felt safe whenever he was with her, and she found herself visiting him more and more each day. Living alone was no longer the life she wanted. She felt the need to be with him. Forever, would she be cautious of the unknown. The desert holds secrets. Not everyone can see them. Tattered scraps of Christine's clothing would later be found in the basement of the Moonbeam Diner by Mr. White's associates. The news further gave Wendy the truth that Johnny had consumed her, and she felt glad to have witnessed his death. She didn't know how long she would feel this way, but it was a feeling that would last for a very long time. It was never determined, but Wendy later made the assumption that Mr. White was working for the secretive organization known as the Men In Black. Although, the existence of such a group has been a topic of debate, and yet to be completely proven. Many people laugh at the idea of their existence, but Wendy was ready to believe in almost anything now. It's to anyone's guess who he truly was, and whom he truly worked for. He quite possibly even worked for himself. Investigating and seeking justice where he deemed necessary. She would never mention his name to people, even if she'd never seen him again. There was no point in doing so. He appeared when he was needed, and left when the job was done.

    Sitting on her bed, Wendy looked out the window of her new bedroom where she watched Mohan and his father working in the cactus gardens. She held a book in her hands along with a pen as she thought to herself. A gentle warm breeze of the day drifted inside and it made her feel refreshed as she breathed it in. Looking down at her diary, she wrote her thoughts down in silence...and then slowly closed the cover.

"If this is life...then mine has only been a dream. For now I know the truth. The world holds secrets all around us...and only few of us can see them. To be paranoid is not an option. This is my reality...but it's sadly not ours. You must look beyond the obvious, because it's there to cloud the mystery."

Author's Notes

While writing this story, it became obvious to me that I had an interest in the New Mexican desert long before I started this. At the time of writing "Moonbeam", I had never been to this area of the United States. I plan to visit it during a trip through Route 66, and to see the city of Roswell along the way. Possibly by the time you have read this, I will have already been there. The town I focused this story on has always interested me. I love the mystery behind it and all the conspiracies. It makes for great storytelling and allows the mind to explore outside of what most consider being natural logic. I almost felt like living there, even temporarily just to allow my imagination to run wild. I've always believed there to be many mysteries surrounding us in life, and many of them will never be fully explored if we don't care to notice.

I probably won't ever live in New Mexico permanently, considering the climate would be rather harsh on my well being. I've always lived in cooler places of the country, and mostly the northern areas. Especially since I'm a lover of snow. Maybe it's one reason why I was drawn to this area of the world for a story, and the stories of Roswell certainly helped fuel my creativity. Having set the theme during the time period featured in my book, felt very fitting for the story itself. I've grown very fond of the characters in this book, and at least one of them I have mentioned before. Readers of my work will certainly recognize this particular person. I can't seem to confine this character to just one story.

All the music mentioned in this book helped give me inspiration while writing those scenes they were featured in. It certainly helped that they were songs I already loved hearing, and I would play them often to complete this work. It took me a year and four months to write "Moonbeam" and it only gave me writer's block for a short time, which I'm thankful. I was able to keep the story in my mind often and hold the inspiration until the end. I'm still feeling it even as I write this, and I can admit that at least one character I wrote in reference to someone close to me in my life. It just goes to show you, that you never know where my mind is going to go next.

I have many stories to tell.

Scott M. Stockton

Printed in Great Britain
by Amazon